"Forget blondes, Taylor. Think brunette!"

Instead of answering the caller, Taylor glared at Rebecca. Clear as anything, he was thinking, *This is all your fault, dammit!*

The next caller was also a woman. "Good evening, Mr. McCoy. I want to tell you about a niece of mine. Now, if anyone can change your mind about marriage, my niece Suzette is the one."

The radio station's telephone lines were buzzing. Rebecca's publicity campaign was certainly starting to take off, although not quite the way she'd anticipated.

Taylor gripped the microphone. "Folks, you seem to be overly interested in my marital status. But it's the marital status of somebody else you ought to be concerned about. I'm referring to a pretty redhead named Rebecca Danley, sitting here beside me in the studio tonight. It so happens Rebecca would like a couple of kids—the problem is she doesn't have a man. What are we going to do about it?"

The next caller was a man....

Ellen James has wanted a writing career ever since she won a national short-story contest when she was in high school. As *The Confirmed Bachelor* is Ellen's ninth Harlequin Romance novel, she obviously has her wish. And be sure to look for Ellen's first Superromance novel, *Tempting Eve*, also available this month.

Books by Ellen James

HARLEQUIN ROMANCE
3154—LOVE'S HARBOR
3202—LOVE YOUR ENEMY
3254—GROWING ATTRACTION
3291—HOME FOR CHRISTMAS
3299—TWO FOR THE HEART

HARLEQUIN SUPERROMANCE
613—TEMPTING EVE

THE CONFIRMED BACHELOR
Ellen James

Harlequin Books

TORONTO • NEW YORK • LONDON
AMSTERDAM • PARIS • SYDNEY • HAMBURG
STOCKHOLM • ATHENS • TOKYO • MILAN
MADRID • WARSAW • BUDAPEST • AUCKLAND

ISBN 0-373-03329-X

THE CONFIRMED BACHELOR

Copyright © 1994 by Ellen James.

All rights reserved. Except for use in any review, the reproduction or
utilization of this work in whole or in part in any form by any electronic,
mechanical or other means, now known or hereafter invented, including
xerography, photocopying and recording, or in any information storage
or retrieval system, is forbidden without the written permission of the
publisher, Harlequin Enterprises Limited, 225 Duncan Mill Road,
Don Mills, Ontario, Canada M3B 3K9.

All characters in this book have no existence outside the imagination of
the author and have no relation whatsoever to anyone bearing the same
name or names. They are not even distantly inspired by any individual
known or unknown to the author, and all incidents are pure invention.

This edition published by arrangement with Harlequin Enterprises B. V.

® and TM are trademarks of the publisher. Trademarks indicated with
® are registered in the United States Patent and Trademark Office, the
Canadian Trade Marks Office and in other countries.

Printed in U.S.A.

CHAPTER ONE

THE MAN WAS PERFECT, absolutely perfect—all six feet two or three inches of him, muscles powerfully outlined by a uniform, hair soft and brown curling from under his cap. He stood alone at home plate, looking out over the baseball diamond with an intense expression on his face. That expression intrigued Rebecca Danley, echoing somehow the odd wistfulness she herself had been feeling these past few weeks. But she didn't stop to analyze the emotions stirred up in her by this man. She only knew that she had to capture him on film. Lifting her camera, she focused through her viewfinder, zoomed in on him and clicked the shutter. Even at this slight sound, he swiveled his head toward Rebecca and stared full at her, a distracted frown taking over his rugged features.

She retreated a little with her camera. From long experience, she knew she obtained her best photographs when she was in the background, and people forgot they were being observed. She moved closer to one of the dugouts and began casually searching through her camera bag for another lens filter. She tried to make it appear as if the man standing at home plate didn't hold even the slightest interest for her. But obviously he had a suspicious nature. He gazed at Rebecca for a long moment, still frowning.

"Ms....uh, whoever you are," he called. "Isn't it a little late for you to be prowling around out here? Game's over. Everybody else has gone home."

"Rebecca Danley," she called back. "And I'm not prowling, I'm doing my job. The light's still good, you know." She made a gesture meant to encompass the entire dome of mellow evening sky curving above the baseball stadium.

The man strode toward her. "What job?" he asked. "And who are you?"

She stared into his dusky gray eyes. "I'm Rebecca Danley—Beck for short—of Danley Public Relations. I've just been hired to handle publicity for the team. I take it you're the manager. Taylor McCoy, isn't it?"

He nodded. "That's me, all right. But I haven't heard anything about any publicist. And I don't see that we need one. Team's doing fine." He took a commanding stance inside the third-base coach's box and surveyed Beck as if she were a rookie player on the team.

"The owner, Mrs. Latham, just hired me," Beck explained. "I'm sure she'll be telling you all about it very soon. I wanted to get a head start on the job, so that's why I came out to the game this afternoon. It was a wonderful game, by the way." She found herself smiling. "The kids selling popcorn and snow cones and peanuts, the organist playing 'Take Me Out to the Ball Game,' the audience yelling and hooting at every excuse. I hadn't been to a ballpark in years, and I'd forgotten how much fun it can be."

Taylor took off his cap and brushed a hand through hair that was attractively sweat-dampened on this warm New Mexico evening. "Tell me, Ms. Danley, did you happen to pay *any* attention to the game itself?"

"Of course. I was impressed by the way your team shut out the opposition. That triple in the third inning really put the Roadrunners ahead—scored two runs. And I especially liked that argument you had with the umpire, bottom of the fifth, when you stormed out of the dugout and kicked dirt all over his shoes."

Now Taylor's face took on a look of reluctant humor. "Yeah, well, you know what they say. Umpires are like kegs of dynamite. Touch one, and they'll blow you right out of the stadium. Just go for their shoes."

"As a matter of fact, I didn't know they say that. But I like the sound of it." Beck fished around in her bag for her notebook. Flipping to a fresh page, she started jotting down the words "Umpires are like kegs of—"

"Wait a minute," said Taylor, craning his neck to see what she was writing.

"Don't worry, Mr. McCoy. I double-check all quotes before printing them. I'm very thorough about my interviews."

"That's exactly what I'm afraid of. Listen, Ms. Danley, I don't know anything about this public-relations scam of yours, but—"

"You might as well call me Rebecca," she said briskly. "You'll be dealing with me quite a lot, after all. Or, if you prefer, call me Beck. Most people do."

He slapped his baseball cap back on his head and adjusted it to a rather grim angle. "I don't give interviews...Beck. Get your quotes from the staff in the front office."

Beck recapped her pen and closed her notebook. "I think you have the wrong idea about my job here. I don't intend just to stay on the surface. I want to get to know the team before I start my publicity campaign. You're instrumental to that, Mr. McCoy. You're the manager—you represent the Roadrunners better than anyone."

She tapped her finger lightly against the shutter of her camera. She had to admit that right now her interest in Taylor McCoy wasn't entirely professional; it didn't all have to do with the publicity campaign ahead of her. Frankly, she suspected the man was going to look great on film. She was *positive* he'd look great. Rarely had she encountered someone who inspired her photographic eye the way Taylor McCoy did. It wasn't only his powerful physique or his undeniably pleasing features. No, it was something more, some depth of emotion she glimpsed in his expressive face. That was what she itched to capture with her camera. Unfortunately it appeared that Taylor McCoy was going to be a difficult subject.

"Listen, Ms. Danley," he said. "Beck—whatever. So happens I was enjoying a quiet moment out here by myself. I don't get to do that very often, and it seems a shame to spoil it. In other words, goodbye."

Beck could no longer resist. Swinging her camera into position, she brought Taylor McCoy's frowning face into focus, adjusted the shutter speed, pulled back a bit on the zoom lens...click. It would be a fine picture, just fine, in spite of Taylor's eloquent scowl.

At the moment, Taylor's scowl seemed just a little *too* eloquent. Beck could easily imagine him grabbing her camera and hurling it into the outfield. Just to be on the safe side, she wrapped the camera strap more snugly around her wrist.

"Mr. McCoy," she said, "has anyone ever told you you're quite photogenic?".

Taylor did not appear mollified by this comment. He looked Beck over, his eyebrows drawn together as if he was considering ways to banish her from the ballpark. He seemed to notice every detail about her: the summery cotton dress she wore, flowered like a country garden, her toes bare in sandals, her strawberry-red hair cropped short but still waving a bit over her forehead. She busied herself with her camera, rewinding the film.

"Mr. McCoy, I'm sorry you don't feel more . . . optimistic about my publicity work. But Mrs. Latham *did* hire me, and I'm going to do a good job for the Roadrunners. I'm going to do my very best job, in fact."

Taylor seemed on the verge of arguing with her, but then a scuffling noise came from behind them, and both Taylor and Beck glanced toward the dugout. A girl of ten or so sat hunched on the bench, looking glum as she dragged the tip of a bat over the ground. Her dark hair was pulled up in a high-flying ponytail, but at the moment even her ponytail seemed to droop. She was dressed in a baseball uniform identical to Taylor's, and after a second Beck recognized her as the Roadrunners' batgirl. All during the game today, this kid had run energetically between home plate and the dugout, retrieving the hitters' bats and returning them to their rack. Beck wondered what could be causing the girl's dejection now, but Taylor seemed to know right off.

"Hey, Jenny," he said. "Didn't I promise you we'd work on your swing today?"

The girl immediately brightened, sitting up straighter. "Yeah, coach, that's what you said."

"Well, get over here, then. Let's practice!"

Grinning, Jenny scrambled out of the dugout and came jogging toward Taylor. He steered her toward home plate, all the while glancing over his shoulder at Beck.

"Goodbye," he said pointedly.

"So long," she answered in her own cheerful tone. She finished rewinding the film in her camera, popped it out and stored it in an empty canister that went straight into her camera bag. And out of her bag she took a new roll of film and threaded it into the camera. Taylor watched these maneuvers for another moment, making it very clear he disliked them. But Jenny was waiting, and at last Taylor gave his full attention to the girl.

"Okay," he said. "Show me your stance. That's what we're going to work on first."

Jenny looked happy. She positioned herself at the plate, feet angled apart.

"Pretty good," Taylor said. "But tell you what—I want you to close up your stance a little. You'll get more power that way because your shoulders will have greater rotation. That's right, feet closer together... square yourself to the plate..."

Taylor seemed completely engrossed in his coaching task. He treated Jenny with an easy respect, as if she were simply another one of the players on his team. Beck had to admire that—and she had to get it on film. And find an angle that would be just right for her shot. The evening light was growing dimmer, and she adjusted her camera's depth of field to compensate. This time Taylor didn't seem to notice the slight sounds she made. Good. She wanted him to forget she was here. She crouched down, took yet another shot and moved again, as stealthy as if photographing a leopard in the jungle.

With his powerful grace, Taylor McCoy reminded her of a leopard. He held the bat up, demonstrating techniques to Jenny.

"See, what I want you to do is choke up a little on the bat, like this," he said, sliding his hands up the polished wood. "Cuts down on the weight you're wielding and gives you more leverage." He took a swing, and Beck could tell this was something he'd been doing all his life, swinging a bat as if it were a natural extension of his arm. But then he winced, stopping to rub his shoulder.

"You okay, coach?" Jenny asked.

"Sure, sure," he muttered. "I'm fine. Now I want you to show me your swing. Hmm . . . not bad, but be sure to follow all the way through the ball. . . ."

Beck focused on Taylor and Jenny. Yes, somehow she had to capture that ease and camaraderie between the two of them. Jenny's ponytail bounced energetically now as she practiced her swing, and once she seemed to laugh with sheer exhilaration. She was full of excitement about baseball, that much was evident. Excited and happy, just the way a kid ought to be. . . .

Beck felt an odd tightness in her throat and had to lower her camera for a minute. This past year or so she'd been thinking about kids a lot, about their un-fettered joyfulness toward life, their curiosity and enthusiasm. At times she'd actually been charmed by their unruliness, too, their stubborn need to push their limits. And when she'd turned twenty-eight a month ago, things had gotten worse. She'd go for a walk and gaze wistfully at kids on skateboards, kids flying kites, kids running home from school with book bags bouncing against their sides. Or Beck would find herself wandering through stores, only to end up in the toy department, fingering doll clothes and jigsaw puzzles, stuffed animals and sets of dominoes. It was becoming downright embarrassing.

Beck fiddled impatiently with her zoom lens. She didn't know the reason for this fascination with children. Even if she wanted a family—kids of her own and all—her life just didn't seem to be moving in that direction. The way Beck figured it, you met a guy, fell in love with him and wanted to have his kids—in that order. She was a diehard romantic and couldn't imagine it any other way. Problem was, she'd gotten things all turned around. She hadn't run across the right guy yet. She'd dated plenty of men, but never one who was interested in starting a family. Yet her fascination with children seemed to grow stronger every day. She had good friends, a great career—but somehow none of that stopped her from ending up in the dratted toy department every time she went to the store.

She bent down again and clicked another picture of Taylor as he patiently coached Jenny. This time perhaps she was too sudden with her movement, because Taylor stopped to glare at her. She stared back at him through her viewfinder. He advanced toward her, looming larger and larger. As he neared, she had to crane her neck back to keep him in focus. She clicked the shutter one more time with a definite sense of satisfaction, Taylor McCoy's face filling the entire lens.

"Don't you have anything better to do than stick a camera in my face?" he grumbled.

"What I really need to do is interview you, Mr. McCoy."

"Interviews," he muttered. "I had damn well enough of interviews when I played in the majors. Thought I'd be done with that kind of garbage now that I'm down here in the bush leagues."

"Albuquerque isn't exactly the bush. And we actually believe 'down here' that publicity can be a good thing. I saw way too many empty seats today, but pretty soon I'll have your attendance up where it belongs."

"Attendance will be up soon enough on its own," Taylor said. "This year the team's headed straight for a league championship. People will start paying notice to that."

"Not if they don't hear about it. And it's my job to make sure they do."

Taylor seemed to deliberate about something, then shook his head. He glanced toward home plate, where Jenny the batgirl still waited hopefully.

"We'll practice some more tomorrow, Jenny. Right now I have to take care of a problem." It was obvious that Taylor considered Beck the problem. He turned back to her and took hold of her elbow. "Let's go to my office, Ms. Danley, and put a stop to all this before it gets out of hand." He steered her among the bleachers, dragging her along like an unwanted sack of baseballs. A moment later he took her down a corridor, banged open a door and drew her unceremoniously into his office.

At least Beck surmised that this impossibly cluttered room was Taylor McCoy's office. Books and magazines were piled everywhere—on the battered desk, on the straight-backed wooden chairs, on the tiled floor. There was a heap of baseball gloves on the floor, too, along with haphazard stacks of tattered file folders. No pictures of any type adorned the greenish walls, but several complicated charts were tacked up here and there, drawn in bold handwriting. Beck stood in the middle of the room, marveling at the unabashed chaos. The place was windowless, and with those green walls it seemed tinged the color of damp seaweed. She raised her camera to get a quick shot.

"Don't even think about it," Taylor commanded. "Have a seat."

Since every available surface was covered with litter, Beck remained standing. Taylor glanced around, then scooped a pile of baseball magazines off one of the chairs.

"I'm still getting settled in," he said. "This is my first season with the Roadrunners."

Somehow Beck suspected Taylor liked his own brand of clutter and would perpetually be in the process of "settling in." But she didn't say anything, merely sat in the chair he'd cleared off. He went behind his desk and threw himself down. Then he reached for the phone and punched out a number, afterward drumming his fingers on one of the few clear spots on the desk. It appeared as if no one was answering his call—but it also appeared that Taylor wasn't going to give up any time soon. Beck took advantage of the opportunity to examine the pile of books and magazines beside her. She saw several back issues of sports publications, a few magazines about horses. There was also a book on cowboys in Hollywood Westerns that looked interesting.

She glanced over at Taylor. He was gripping the telephone receiver and frowning at her. She smiled back at him to prove *she* bore no hard feelings. Her smile wasn't infectious, however; Taylor McCoy's frown only deepened.

At last it seemed he'd coerced someone to pick up the other end of the line.

"Hello?" he said. "Is that you, Alma? Look, we have to discuss this publicity person you've got prowling around... That's right, I said prowling. Uh...thanks, it *was* a good game. Looks like we've got a real hitter on our hands with Stan Parker... Anyway, Alma, what's with this publicity lady? Beck Danley, she calls herself. She's too damn camera-happy, and she wants to run all over the place doing interviews. Why didn't you tell me anything about her?"

Beck's finger twitched on the shutter of her camera. She was tempted to snap another photograph, just to annoy Taylor. Here he was, arguing about her with Alma Latham, owner of the New Mexico Roadrunners.

"...Look, Alma, the guys have been shook up enough this year. First you bought the team, then you hired me as new manager. Everybody's just starting to get used to all the changes, but that's exactly my point. Now that we're headed for the championship, I don't want any more turmoil. And Beck Danley is turmoil, I can see that much already.''

For Pete's sake, he was making her sound like a hurricane showing up on a weatherman's radar screen. She glared at Taylor, but he went right on talking to Mrs. Latham.

"She's trouble, Alma, I can sense it. Hmm...but I don't do interviews...yeah...uh-huh...all right, dammit, I'll consider it. But it's the only thing I'm willing to do.'' Taylor thumped the receiver down and stared at Beck with an expression of unmitigated disgust.

"Alma thinks you're the best thing to hit this stadium since Crackerjacks. You must have given her some sales pitch, Danley.''

"I'm sure you gave her a sales pitch yourself when you were hired to manage this team. And I was hired to publicize the team. What's so terrible about that?''

Still looking dissatisfied, he leaned back in his chair. "I just don't want my team disrupted, that's all. Picture it this way. You don't change your swing when your batting average is high and you're in the middle of a winning streak. And the Roadrunners are right smack in the middle of a winning streak. Hell, I don't even want my players changing the socks they wore when they made their last home run. So I sure don't want them thinking about some pretty redhead all of a sudden, or posing to have their pictures taken.''

Taylor McCoy's tone made "pretty redhead" sound like an insult, but she couldn't help being a little pleased.

"Mr. McCoy, I'm very businesslike when it comes to my job. Do you honestly think I'd try to distract your players?"

He kept drumming his fingers on his cluttered desk. "You'll distract them all right, just by being around. I've seen it happen before. When I was playing short-stop in the majors, Tom Walters was knocking in two or three runs a game, taking us straight to the World Series. Then old Tom started mooning about some blonde reporter who kept wanting to interview him. Next thing you knew, his batting average went down the toilet. I don't want that happening with my players. I don't want them looking at those blue eyes and that red hair of yours, and have their minds start to wander. Do I have to make myself any clearer, *Ms*. Danley?"

She smoothed back a strand of the wavy red hair that threatened to cause Taylor McCoy so much grief. "This all sounds awfully superstitious to me. I mean, if you literally don't want your players to change their socks..."

"All good ball players are superstitious, Beck. It's part of the game. I once knew a pitcher who ate the exact same breakfast every morning for ten years—corn flakes and carrot juice—because that's what he'd had before a no-hitter in Milwaukee. You could say it was all in his head, and you'd probably be right. But that's the power of superstition, and I don't believe in bucking it."

She gazed at him skeptically. "You're handing me a line, Mr. McCoy. Something tells me this isn't just about baseball superstitions. What else is going on here?"

His face took on a closed look. "That's the problem with you publicity people. You're always trying to find out things you have no business knowing."

Beck raised both hands in exasperation. "I don't know who you've dealt with before, but in case you don't realize it, a publicist's job is to protect her clients, not exploit them. I'm the one who acts as a buffer between you and the media. I'm the one who makes sure they print only what you want, and—"

"A noble profession, your public relations," he said caustically. "But you don't need to give me any more justifications for what you do. Alma Latham asked me to grant you one short interview, and I'll do that much. So ask your questions, Beck Danley, and let's get the thing over with."

Stifling a curse, Beck pulled out her notebook again. From the very beginning Taylor McCoy had put her on the defensive, made her feel that she had to defend what she did for a living. But she was proud of her work. Most of her clients considered her a friend, someone who believed in and nurtured their dreams. That was why she'd ventured into public relations in the first place—she was good at capturing the vision of other people's dreams. And she did everything she could to portray her visions effectively, whether her client was a singer in a country-western band, a stand-up comic or a would-be magician.

Beck didn't think Taylor McCoy would understand any of this. She was no longer in any mood to interview the man. But work was work; she'd promised Alma Latham she would do her very best by the

Roadrunners. She uncapped her pen and turned to a fresh page in her notebook.

"All right, Mr. McCoy, let's get right down to business. Question number one—are you married?"

CHAPTER TWO

TAYLOR MCCOY'S REACTION to Beck's question was not overwhelmingly positive.

"What in blazes does it matter whether or not I'm married?" he demanded. "You're supposed to ask me about things like my number of career home runs, not my marital status."

Beck drew a sketch in her notebook—a caricature of a stubborn-jawed man, topping it with a baseball cap. She gave the face a healthy grimace, too. "Unfortunately, Mr. McCoy, the public wants to know more about you than numbers. It wants to know what you do in your spare time, how you feel about your career, whether you have a steady girl—"

"The public doesn't want to know any of those things. The public couldn't care less. *You're* the one who wants to know, Ms. Danley."

She gave the caricature some well-formed ears. "Believe me, it's nothing personal. I'm just trying to figure out the best way to present you in the press releases. If you'd cooperate, you could help me a great deal."

"Ms. Danley—"

"I'm just doing my job," she said implacably.

It was obvious Taylor meant to delay as long as possible. He shifted in his chair. He thumped his fingers on the desk, then slapped his way through a pile of decrepit file folders. But at last he gave in.

"Definitely not married. Satisfied?"

Beck drew some soft wisps of hair under the baseball cap of her impromptu portrait. "You sound rather adamant on the subject."

"I am. Next question."

Beck gave her portrait a strong, well-defined neck. She smiled a little, an idea beginning to percolate in her brain. Perhaps a very good idea.

"Mr. McCoy, let's stick to the subject of marriage for a bit. Don't you see any possibility of it in your future?"

Taylor slapped through the file folders one more time. "Ms. Danley, I already answered the question. Let's move on."

"Yes, but I'm trying to understand your attitude here. Are you completely opposed to the state of matrimony, or is it simply a matter of—"

"Listen, I don't need a wife, just like I don't need this damn interview." Taylor leaned toward her, pushing aside the folders so he could prop his elbows on the desk. "I don't see how I can make it any clearer than that. No wife. That stands for now and the foreseeable future. Next question!"

Beck gave her portrait some muscled arms. "Let me guess. Your dating strategy is just like your baseball strategy. Don't change your swing when your batting average is high."

Taylor considered this, and then nodded. "Not bad, Ms. Danley. Not bad at all."

Beck tapped her pen thoughtfully against her notebook. After a few moments she gave her sketch some powerful legs and some cleated shoes. Portrait complete—except for a title. Underneath she jotted down, "Baseball's Most Confirmed Bachelor." She ripped out the sheet of paper and handed it to Taylor.

"What do you think? See any resemblance?"

He looked the caricature over. "So now you're an artist, too. But my ears can't possibly be that big. You'd better stick to photography."

Beck stood up, swinging her bag over her shoulder and popping the lens cap back on her camera. "Guess that about does it. Thanks for the interview."

"That's it? One lousy question?"

"That's it." She reached across and shook his hand in a firm grasp. "Mr. McCoy, you've given me everything I need. Goodbye for now. And thanks again." She strode out of his office, humming a little under her breath. She could swear she felt one of Taylor's disapproving frowns follow her all the way down the corridor, but she didn't turn around to find out for sure. She grinned as she went along the concourse of the stadium. She was anxious to really get started with her work.

COMPLETE BLACKNESS muffled the small room like a rich soft blanket. Beck couldn't see a thing, but she worked deftly, winding film onto a reel in her hand. She loved this darkroom of hers and considered it the most important part of her office. She spent countless enjoyable hours here, processing film and making prints. The work soothed her, as if closing the door and turning out the lights really did wrap her in a warm soft blanket. The past few days she'd been in extra need of some soothing; the job with the New

Mexico Roadrunners was turning out to be far more hectic than she'd anticipated.

She slipped the reel of film into a small round processing tank. She sighed happily and settled into her work, but only a few moments later her relaxation was disturbed by a knock on the darkroom door.

"Rebecca? Dammit, Rebecca, are you in there?" came Taylor McCoy's voice.

For crying out loud, what was *he* doing here? Beck had avoided him as much as possible since their first meeting at the baseball stadium. And he had made a special effort to avoid her, too, as if he had an allergic reaction to her camera. What could he possibly want from her now?

Beck was tempted not to answer him. She could stay here cloaked in her comfortable darkness, and perhaps he'd give up and go away. But he rapped on the door again.

"I know you're in there. Come on out. You have a hell of a lot of explaining to do!"

Goodness, he sounded riled. And he probably *wouldn't go away.* Still moving unerringly in the dark, Beck placed the lid on the processing tank and then switched on one of the safelights to cast a muted glow in the room. She turned to open the door, but then hesitated. This place was her personal sanctuary. She had everything ordered just the way she liked it: a trim row of processing trays, neatly labeled beakers for all her chemical solutions, a systematic arrangement of photo easels, printing frames, sponges and clips. When so much of her work was done in total darkness or dim light, she had to be orderly. After seeing the vibrant chaos of Taylor's office, she feared he'd bring some of that chaos whirling in here.

He banged on the door again. "Rebecca!"

"Okay, already." She swung the door open and glared at him. "I'm busy, McCoy. My secretary works mornings—call her early tomorrow and make an appointment if you want to see me."

Taylor charged into the room, waving a newspaper at her. "Supposedly you're my publicist. Why should I have to make an appointment to see my own publicist? Especially after this bunk you had printed about me!"

Beck glanced at the newspaper he'd thrust under her nose. "I gather you've read this morning's edition of the *Courier*," she said with satisfaction. "The sports editor devoted an entire two pages to the Roadrunners. I was very pleased to get that kind of coverage."

"I damn well wasn't pleased to get it," Taylor said grimly. "The whole thing's about me, not about the team. You're supposed to be covering the team." He rattled the newspaper, and Beck could imagine the entire room beginning to rattle with agitation just from Taylor's presence.

"Every word in that newspaper article was deliberately chosen to promote the Roadrunners," she said. "It just so happens that you're the heart of the team. Whenever I interview the players, they end up talking about you—how you're the one who's motivating everybody for a run at the championship. Even when I interviewed Jenny the batgirl, all she could talk about was how you take the time to coach her and how you encourage her by telling her that someday women will be playing in the league. So of course you're the focus of the article."

"I want the focus changed. I had enough publicity in the majors to last me ten lifetimes." Taylor snapped open the newspaper, scowling at the sports section. "And what's with all these photographs of me? It looks like you practically followed me into the locker room with your camera."

Beck studied the newspaper. "You're overreacting. I selected two photos of you for this article. Count 'em two. That other picture only shows Jenny your back's to the camera, so it doesn't really count." Beck didn't mention that Taylor had a very appealing backside that showed up well in the photograph; she didn't think he'd appreciate it. She quickly pointed to the last photo in the layout. "Now, this is a shot of the team. Granted, you *are* in the background, but you're far enough away that no one can see you grimacing at the camera, so this one doesn't count, either."

Taylor smacked the newspaper shut. "Okay, Rebecca, I'll tell you what really sticks in my craw the most—the way you've announced to the entire population of New Mexico that I'm baseball's most confirmed bachelor. What kind of label is that to slap on me?"

Beck went to one of the counters and dipped a thermometer into her developer fluid to check for proper temperature. Taylor sounded so worked up she suspected his own temperature was shooting dangerously high. "I don't see what the problem is. You told me yourself that you *are* baseball's most confirmed bachelor. It's a great angle, guaranteed to intrigue women all across the state. Wait and see, McCoy—this is going to be some publicity campaign, and it's all thanks to you." She smiled and poured developer into the processing tank.

Taylor groaned, pushing back the faded Red Sox baseball cap he wore. "I don't believe this. We were just talking that first day. It wasn't supposed to be something you took seriously!"

Beck started briskly shaking the tank with one hand, glancing over at Taylor with interest. "You mean you really aren't a confirmed bachelor? That'll make New Mexico women even happier."

Taylor's eyebrows drew together. "Dammit, of course I'm a confirmed bachelor. I have good reason to be."

"What reason? I mean, as your publicist, maybe it's something I ought to know about. So I can make sure it doesn't get into print if you don't want it there."

He dropped the newspaper on the counter. "Are you trying to tell me you're actually concerned about my welfare?"

"Well, of course. I'm concerned about the welfare of all my clients. I was very careful with that article. Believe me, you come across as a wonderful person. All your players admire you. It's very inspiring. Saying that you're a confirmed bachelor just adds a nice, warm human touch."

Taylor took a step to plant himself right in front of her. His gray eyes were dark as cinder. "I don't want to come across as a wonderful person. I want my private life to be just that—private. And I intend to keep it like that."

Beck couldn't look away from his eyes. Belatedly she realized that she was forgetting to shake the processing tank; heaven knew how this poor film was going to turn out. She jiggled the tank upside down, then rapped it against the counter to pop any air bubbles inside. Around Taylor she couldn't seem to think straight, as if her head was filling up with air bubbles, for goodness' sake!

"Look, Mr. McCoy...Taylor. I think you've made it very clear how you feel about me and the work I do. But you have to realize I was hired to promote the team, and I'll do whatever I see fit to accomplish that."

"I sure hope those aren't more pictures of me you're fooling with right now."

Beck drained out the developer and poured in some bleach. She cranked on her timer, even though it probably wouldn't do her any good to keep going. "Don't worry," she said. "These *were* pictures of you and the team, but I've no doubt ruined them. You're too distracting in here."

He didn't take this not-so-subtle suggestion that he leave. Instead, he perused the prints she'd tacked to a corkboard on the wall. Shots of different team members and, yes, more shots of Taylor himself. Beck winced in preparation for another protest from him. No protest came. Taylor merely examined a picture that showed him twisting in the air to catch a fly ball. Beck was particularly proud of that photo. It captured all of Taylor's power and gracefulness and at the same time captured his intense, almost sorrowful expression, too, as if, somehow, catching that ball had given him sadness, as well as joy.

Taylor stared at the photograph for a long silent moment, and his expression became almost an echo of

the one he wore in the picture. He reached up to rub
his shoulder. Beck had seen him do that before; many
of the Roadrunners had spoken sympathetically about
how Taylor had lost his career as a ball player due to
a shoulder injury. But she didn't question Taylor
about it. His rigid stance made it clear he would tolerate no further incursions into his private life, even if
those incursions were made by his well-meaning publicist. Perhaps *especially* if they were made by his well-
meaning publicist.

Beck's timer went off, and both she and Taylor gave
a start. To her chagrin, she realized she'd been gog-
gling at Taylor again and had forgotten to shake the
processing tank. She had no hope left at all for her
film, but she hurried to the sink, anyway, and began
rinsing water through the tank. Meanwhile, Taylor
looked at the other photographs tacked to the corkboard.

"Lots of pictures of kids," he observed.

For some reason Beck felt defensive. "The reason I
have so many pictures of kids is because one of my
clients is a clown."

"A clown?"

"That's right, a very experienced and professional
clown who performs at children's birthday parties.
You can see him in the pictures, over there—and there.
Anyway, of course I have to do a lot of publicity shots
of him, and of the kids, to show how well he's entertaining them, so that's why there're so many pictures
of kids. I mean, it's not like that's all I do. I don't just
take pictures of kids!" Beck drew a deep breath and
tried unsuccessfully to relax. She couldn't very well

explain to Taylor about this untimely fascination she'd developed for children of all sizes and shapes.

Taylor gave her a quizzical look, but didn't say anything. He folded his arms, leaned against the counter and surveyed her as carefully as he had her photographs. She tried to concentrate on the remaining steps of her film processing, the fixer and stabilizer fluids waiting in their water bath for her to get on with things. But with Taylor watching her and not saying a word, she felt all turned around. Why wouldn't this impossible man just leave? Under his scrutiny, she had to set her timer twice before she got it right. And now she was shaking the tank way too much; it almost flew out of her hand.

What was Taylor looking at, anyway? She went to the clothesline strung across one corner of the darkroom, took a clip and hung up her poor abused film to dry. She gave the film a cursory swipe with a sponge, and mentally apologized for being so slipshod. She also mentally placed the blame right smack on Taylor McCoy. Then she marched out to the main area of her office, grateful when Taylor followed her. Perhaps in less-confined quarters, he wouldn't affect her so much. But she hadn't counted on him snooping around out here, too. He immediately gravitated toward the wooden rocking horse that she'd pushed away in one corner.

"Hey, this is really something," he said. "A good old-time horse. Look at the detailed carving."

"Yes, it's quite impressive, isn't it? That's why I couldn't pass it up in the store the other day. It's sort of...sort of a curio. It doesn't mean anything special. I just...well, I pictured how it would look, some kid riding it, pretending to be a cowboy. Or a cowgirl, as the case may be. The image stuck in my mind, that's all...." She was being defensive again, and Taylor was looking at her with more curiosity than ever. Why couldn't she keep her mouth shut? There was no sensible way to explain why she'd started buying things like rocking horses and stuffed animals. She moved protectively in front of the bookshelf where she'd tucked away a stuffed koala bear. That was a mistake; she only drew Taylor's attention. He picked up the bear and dangled it by one plump, fuzzy little paw.

"You like toys, Rebecca? Maybe you're buying presents for a niece or nephew."

He'd given her an easy out, but she'd never been good at lying. She snatched the koala bear away from him and crammed it back on the shelf.

"I don't have nieces or nephews," she muttered. "My brother's married, but he doesn't have any kids. I just bought some toys, that's all. It's a perfectly natural thing to do...."

Taylor gave the rocking horse a nudge. It rocked back and forth in a most pleasing manner, but Beck wished she could throw a towel over it. And she wished that Taylor McCoy would just go.

"Goodbye, Taylor," she said.

"So long," he returned casually, but he'd seen something else on the bookshelf that interested him. He picked up a catalog Beck had recently acquired. *"Babies Unlimited,"* he read aloud. "'Everything the new parent needs, and more.'"

Beck tried to grab the catalog away from him, but he dodged her easily, flipping through the pages. "Swings...high chairs...carriages. Hey, this baby carriage looks like it has its own motor. The kid could be driving before he's even three.''

At last Beck managed to snatch the catalog away from him. She tossed it into the trash can. "Bunch of clutter," she said, then glanced pointedly at her watch. "Good*bye*, Taylor."

He remained standing right where he was. "All those pictures of kids, toys lying around, mail-order baby catalogs... Doesn't take a genius to figure it out." He looked perturbed. "You should've said something, Rebecca. If I'd known about your, uh, condition, I would've treated you a little differently. Dammit, I wouldn't have hollered at you."

It took Beck a second to realize what he was talking about. She gave a strangled laugh. "You think I'm pregnant?"

He looked at her cautiously. "Maybe you should sit down or something. I could get you a glass of water."

Beck shook her head. "Taylor, a pregnant woman doesn't suddenly become fragile. She's doing something perfectly healthy and normal and wonderful...." With an effort, she stopped herself. She really was a goner if she was uttering a paean to pregnancy; all her friends who'd ever stumbled through morning sickness ought to hear her now. What had gotten into her? "Anyway," she continued forcefully, "I'm *not* expecting. These kid and baby things, they're just..." Beck shrugged, at a loss how to explain.

Taylor smiled slowly. "Hmm, pictures of kids, stuffed toys, that rocking horse... yet you're not pregnant. What's going on with you, Rebecca?"

"If I *knew* what was going on, then I wouldn't be in a fix, would I? I wouldn't be surrounded by all this stuff!'' Beck gave the rocking horse a good nudge of her own. ''It's very inconvenient,'' she grumbled. ''I keep hanging around toy stores. I keep buying stuffed bears and marbles and building blocks. Pretty soon I'll be able to open my *own* toy store.''

''Now that's a thought. Maybe you're looking for a career change and you just haven't admitted it yet.''

Beck gave him a sharp glance. ''Don't get your hopes up, Taylor. I'm not leaving the publicity field anytime soon. I love what I do for a living. This isn't about my career at all. It's about...I don't know what it's about, that's the whole point. I can't explain why I see kids everywhere I go these days. Ten-year-olds on their paper routes, eight-year-olds playing hopscotch, five-year-olds learning how to ride their bikes, for goodness' sake.''

''Hmm, this is all starting to make sense. It reminds me of when I decided to buy a horse. Spent all my time learning about saddles and snaffle bits and hoof picks. Started hanging around stables and racetracks. Got so I noticed horses more than people. Just like you notice kids all the time.''

''You're not being helpful. Really, you aren't.''

''Sure I am.'' Taylor nodded at her as if he'd just discovered a technique to boost her batting average. ''I've got your problem figured out. It's a piece of cake when you know how to read the signs. The toys, the pictures of kids, the way you see children everywhere you go. Yep, the signs are there, all right. You, Rebecca, are suffering from a classic case of baby hunger.''

CHAPTER THREE

BECK STARED at Taylor for long seconds. Again she considered outright lying, but dismissed the thought. "If you really want the truth, McCoy, I wouldn't know what to do with a baby if one fell in my lap!"

"That's not what your photographs say, or this stuffed bear or the rocking horse. You're hankering for a baby. You've got the itch, and you've got it bad."

Beck sank into a chair, struggling with a whole variety of emotions. Taylor's verdict was close to the truth, but not entirely on the mark. Eight- or nine-year-olds, those were the children who drew Beck irrevocably. Babies, on the other hand, were something of a mystery to her. She understood now why she'd picked up that embarrassing catalog the other day. She'd been trying, in some small fashion, to unravel the mystery of babies, as if, by studying all the baby accoutrements, she'd figure out what gave infants their particular appeal. After all, if you were going to have a nine-year-old kid, you'd have to start at the very beginning, with diapers and midnight feedings....

Beck stood up rather quickly. "It's all so ridiculous!" she burst out. "Everything's out of whack. It's like somebody handed me a train schedule for the wrong station. What on earth am I going to do?"

Taylor prodded her back into her chair. "First thing you ought to do is sit down," he said. Then he went to the water cooler in the corner of the office, filled a paper cup and brought it over to her. "Drink," he commanded. "Trust me, it'll help."

She sipped the cool water and found that, indeed, it had a salutary effect. She calmed down enough to wonder why she was spilling all her secrets to Taylor McCoy. But it was too late now; they were spilled. And he seemed to be having a fine time analyzing them. He sat across from her, stretching out his legs comfortably.

"Okay, so what's really the problem here? You want kids, so marry some guy, have kids. Or don't get married, if you don't want to. Just have the kid. Hell, there are plenty of single mothers out there, and they're doing a good job of it."

"But you don't understand. I've never wanted to raise a child on my own. When the time's right, I want to meet someone special and fall in love. The children will come along after. I'm too much of a romantic to have it any other way."

"Hmm, I get it. First comes love, then comes marriage... then comes Becky with a baby carriage."

She gave him a withering glance, which seemed to have no effect.

"So, Rebecca. It seems what you really need is a husband. Any boyfriends at the moment?"

"I'm not dating anyone in particular, if that's what you're asking. Not that you should be asking."

"Just trying to be logical about this. Too bad you're going through a dry spell with dating. That complicates things."

Beck sputtered. "I'm not exactly going through a dry spell. I go to parties, I go on dates."

"Ever meet any husband material?"

"I'm not looking for any!"

"There's your problem. You have to take control of things. You have to be out there looking. You need to find a man, and not just any man. You need to find one who has bona fide father potential."

"Oh, sure, right. I'll just go out there and rope myself an *un*confirmed bachelor, all for the sake of progeny. It doesn't work that way. You can't force romance."

"Looks like we have a problem, then. A real dilemma. Because you've got the kid urge now. In other words, you've got the carriage but not the horse. You've got the caboose but no engine. You've got—"

"I'd like to run *your* caboose right out of here." Beck finished her water in one gulp, crumpled up the cup and tossed it into the trash on top of the baby catalog. "My personal life isn't on the agenda here. I'm supposed to be busy promoting the team, so that's what I'm going to do." Feeling a welcome decisiveness, Beck vacated her chair and strode to the area of her office where she kept a camera mounted on a tripod. The camera faced a background screen of amber cloth. "Now and then I like to take a more formal portrait of my clients. Come on over here, McCoy."

For a moment she almost thought he was going to cooperate. He stood and came to her side, but then he bent to peer through the viewfinder, swiveling the camera toward her.

"What do you say I take a picture of you, instead, Rebecca? Photographers never have pictures of themselves around, you ever notice that? It doesn't seem fair."

"I don't have anything to publicize. You do." Beck readjusted the camera and steered Taylor toward the backdrop, trailing her remote shutter release with her. This way, as soon as she got Taylor positioned correctly, she could snap a photo without having to hurry back to the camera. She'd get her portrait of Taylor before he knew what hit him.

"Hold on a minute," he said, a grin starting on his face. "I think you do have something to publicize. You need a man in your life before this baby hunger gets out of hand. We could mount an all-out publicity campaign to find just the right guy."

Beck frowned at him. "Very funny."

"Hey, I'm serious. I think it could work."

"Wonderful. Why don't I just mail-order myself a husband, the way I'd mail-order one of those cribs or high chairs? You keep forgetting I'm a romantic. No romance—no man. That's the way it has to be for me." She got Taylor in front of the backdrop, but didn't trust him to stay there for more than a second. She was about to press her thumb on the remote button when he tilted her chin gently with one finger.

"Not so fast," he said. "We already have plenty of pictures of me. We need one of you, Rebecca—one showing that glimmer of romance you have in your eyes."

"You're making fun of me, McCoy. You're trying to get revenge for the way I portrayed you in the newspaper."

"I just think it's time you put yourself in front of the camera, that's all. How about an action photo?"

With just a hint of a smile, Taylor bent his head and kissed her. It was a teasing kiss, surely humorous and carefree on his part. And, to her consternation, Taylor squeezed the remote release in her hand. Her thumb came down on the button and *click!* She'd taken a picture. She'd actually taken a picture of Taylor McCoy kissing her! She felt his lips curve against hers before he stepped back.

"Darn it all, McCoy—"

"Maybe I should go into photography, Rebecca. Can't wait to get a few copies of that shot." He strolled to the door, but turned back for a moment, angling his baseball cap lower over his forehead. "As a matter of fact," he said, "better make it a dozen copies of that shot. No, two dozen eight-by-tens and a few wallet-size, just for good measure. And, Rebecca, don't worry. I'm going to help you solve this kid problem of yours. I might even be able to find you a little romance along the way."

He was out the door and gone before Beck could grab her stuffed koala bear and hurl it at him. He was gone all right, leaving her in even greater turmoil than before. It was bad enough having this so-called baby hunger—but now she had to contend with Taylor McCoy's jokes, as well! Worst of all...she had to contend with his kisses.

IT WAS FRIDAY EVENING, and the freeway was clogged bumper to bumper from the five-o'clock rush. Beck signaled, pulled onto the exit ramp and a few moments later drove her small sports coupe into the parking lot of KQIZ Radio.

A big old pickup came jouncing into the parking lot like an ornery bull. It rattled to a stop right next to Beck's car. She peered out her window and saw that the truck was a 1950s' model, with expansive fenders and a curved hood. It was painted apple green, a color that managed to show here and there through generous spatters of mud. The truck looked as if it had been plowing down rutted country roads for the past forty years or so and had only ended up in this city parking lot by mistake.

Taylor McCoy swung down from the truck and came over to Beck's window. This evening he wore a tan jacket that made his hair look dark and rich by contrast. He propped his elbow on the car door and leaned down to smile in at Beck.

"Hello there, Rebecca. This is a great machine you have here. But right away I see a problem. A two-seater isn't exactly a family vehicle, now, is it? Where are you going to stash the kids?"

Beck cursed the moment she'd ever opened her mouth around Taylor McCoy. She hadn't seen him since that mortifying day in her office, and yet instinctively he knew how to provoke her. She glanced over at his pickup.

"You're not exactly driving a family vehicle, either."

"I don't know... I could pile a bunch of the little tykes in the back and do just fine. But I'm a confirmed bachelor, so they tell me. I don't have to worry about these practical details the way you do. I'm not the one who has a bad case of baby hunger."

Beck clenched her hands on the wheel. "Would you stop using that term? If the time is ever suitable for me to have children, I'll certainly buy a larger car. Until then, this car suits me just fine." Beck refused to admit that lately she'd developed an alarming hankering for station wagons. She could well imagine what Taylor would say if he got hold of *that* bit of information.

He seemed to be settling in comfortably at her window. "You know, Rebecca, I don't think we should leave your situation to chance. I really could help you find just the right guy to solve your problem. A romantic, fatherly type all in one—"

Beck cranked up her window and thought longingly about speeding from the parking lot. But this was a work night for her, and she couldn't leave. She was forced to deal with Taylor McCoy. Pushing her door open, she obliged him to step out of the way. Slamming the door shut again, she turned to face him.

"Taylor, your tactics are too obvious. You're trying to make yourself so annoying I won't want to focus my campaign on you. It just won't work. You're my key to promoting the Roadrunners. No matter how obnoxious you become, you'll keep on being the key. The job is just too important to let you get to me."

"You sound mighty determined about this. Are you always so dedicated to your work?"

"I like to help my clients' dreams come true. The Roadrunners mean a lot to Alma Latham. She wants to share the fun of baseball with as many people as possible. Plus, she'd like the team to turn a decent profit so she can afford higher wages for players, improvements at the stadium—that sort of thing. It's her dream, and it's up to me to do something about it. So let's get started, McCoy." She strode past him, leading the way into KQIZ Radio.

She walked briskly down the corridor of the building, waving a greeting to the young receptionist. But the receptionist didn't even appear to see Beck; instead, the woman's gaze followed Taylor as if she were a ship at sea on a foggy night and he was a lighthouse beacon. This confirmed Beck's original suspicion that Taylor McCoy was unnaturally attractive to women of all ages. His attractiveness could be a big asset in promoting the Roadrunners, but right now it irritated Beck. Couldn't the receptionist stop ogling Taylor for even a second?

Taylor himself seemed impervious to the admiration he'd evoked. He walked along beside Beck and found a whole new subject with which to aggravate her.

"I see you didn't bring your camera. Develop any film lately, Rebecca?"

"Of course. I've always got one project or another going in my darkroom."

"Any picture you want to share with me? I'm turning out to be a great fan of photography."

Beck knew exactly what he was referring to—the photograph he'd snapped right in the middle of that kiss. She hadn't been able to bring herself to develop that particular roll of film. Nor had she been able to throw it out, the way she should—even if it meant the waste of an entire roll. Finally she'd buried the film deep in one of the cubbyholes of her desk. She had no idea what she was going to do with it, no idea at all.

Beck was relieved to reach the office of Faye Alvarado, host of KQIZ's premier talk show. Faye, a no-

nonsense woman of fifty or so, gave Taylor a frank inspection.

"Baseball's most confirmed bachelor, am I right? Too bad this isn't television. You look even better in person than you did in those newspaper photos."

Taylor gave Beck an accusing stare. "I'm here to talk about the team, not about myself. That's the only reason I agreed to do this show for Ms. Danley."

Beck smiled back imperturbably at Taylor. "My campaign's working already."

Taylor looked displeased as Faye escorted them into a booth at the broadcast center. A short while later the "KQIZ Quiz Hour" went on the air. Faye was a relaxed, knowledgeable host guaranteed to put even the most recalcitrant guest at ease. But once Taylor began discussing his team, he needed no prompting. He spoke with enthusiasm about base hits and tip fouls, gesturing to demonstrate a pitcher throwing a fast ball, even though the radio audience couldn't see him.

Beck sat in a chair a little off to the side and watched. The man loved baseball; there could be no doubt about that. It was his passion for the game that made him so appealing. And his voice was deep and warm.

"...the little things about baseball, those are unique," he was saying. "A true baseball fan enjoys the little things, looks out for them. The umpire with his whisk, bending down to sweep off the plate, the hitter chewing gum and twirling his bat to warm up, a ball sailing into the stands now and then for some lucky kid to catch. I don't care what anyone tells you, there's nothing grandiose about baseball. It's all on a small scale, the way it ought to be."

Beck became enthusiastic just listening to him. Taylor was describing exactly how she felt about photography. She didn't care for big panoramas. Instead, she liked focusing in on the little things, the small moments of life that too often went unnoticed: a spider weaving its web, water shimmering in the sunlight. She and Taylor gazed at each other, and it seemed to Beck that even without words they were sharing something. Even without speaking to each other, they shared their belief that it was the little things in life that counted most.

Faye asked Taylor another question, and he had to glance away. Soon the interview portion of the show ended, and it was time to accept telephone calls from listeners.

"Hello, Taylor!" sang a female voice over the wire. "I read about you in the newspaper. I know you think you're a confirmed bachelor, but have you tried brunettes? Forget blondes, Taylor. Think brunette!"

Instead of answering the caller, he looked at Beck with an ominous expression. Once again they shared an unspoken message. Clear as anything, Taylor was thinking, *This is all your fault, dammit, Rebecca.*

She lifted her shoulders and smiled at him. *Enjoy yourself,* she sent back. But her own telepathic message didn't seem to get through to him at all. His expression only grew more ominous.

The next caller was also a woman. "Good evening, Mr. McCoy. I want to tell you about a niece of mine. She's very attractive, just graduated from college, and she loves baseball. Now, if anyone can change your mind about marriage, my niece Suzette is the one."

Taylor hunched over the microphone and scowled down at it. "Ma'am, if you want to ask me any questions about the team, I'd be more than happy to answer them."

"I do have one question. Can I give you Suzette's phone number?"

Soon the station's telephone lines were buzzing. A breathless lady announced that she was the solution for Taylor's bachelorhood. A grandmother explained that she had three granddaughters of dating age, but failing that, *she* was available for a date. A thirty-year-old divorcée proclaimed herself a confirmed bachelorette and thus the perfect companion for Taylor. By this time, he looked positively dangerous. Beck pushed her chair back against the wall at what she considered a safe distance from him. The calls continued to pour in. Beck's publicity campaign was really taking off, although not quite the way she'd anticipated.

"Taylor, dear," said the next caller, "being a bachelor is like being sick. There's always a cure, as long as you're willing to work hard at it. Don't ever give up hope."

Taylor gripped the microphone as if about to yank it from its moorings. He stared right at Beck, even as he spoke to the radio audience. "Folks, you seem to be overly interested in my marital status. But it's the marital status of somebody else you ought to be concerned about. I'm referring to a pretty redhead named Rebecca Danley, sitting here beside me in the studio tonight. It so happens Rebecca would like a couple of kids, but the problem is she doesn't have a man. What are we going to do about it?"

Beck jumped up from her chair, almost toppling it over. How could he do this to her? It was mortifying! It was infuriating!

The next caller was a man—a rather harried-sounding man. "Rebecca, I'm a widowed father of five. I'd really like to meet you. My kids would like to meet you—Thomas, stop trying to cook your sister's hair!" A muffled crash came over the wire, followed by several disturbing thuds, and a loud "Ouch!" There was a prolonged silence, and then the father of five surfaced again, like a deep-sea diver coming up for air. "Rebecca ... hello, Rebecca! Are you there?"

While Beck fumed, Taylor settled back leisurely, no longer behaving as if he'd like to strangle the microphone. No matter. Beck would gladly have strangled it for him.

The next caller was also a man. "Rebecca, I'm interested in starting a family myself. But I'm sure you realize how important heredity is. I have an excellent genetic makeup, and I'd like to find out if your genes are compatible. Perhaps we could discuss chromosomal analysis...."

Forget strangling the microphone. Beck was ready to strangle Taylor. More aunts and grandmothers called in, but now they were advertising nephews and grandsons, instead of nieces and granddaughters. Beck had thoroughly had it with the "KQIZ Quiz Hour." She didn't think she could tolerate one more second. And at last she was free. Mercifully the show ended, although the switchboard was still lit up with calls from people who either wanted to save Taylor from bachelorhood or Beck from nonparenthood.

Beck strode out of the building and into the warm shadows of dusk. She fumbled with her car door, only to have Taylor come up behind her.

"I thought it turned out to be a damn good show," he remarked. "All things considered, that is."

Beck whirled around to confront him. "You turned the entire thing into a humiliating joke! I made the mistake of telling you something about myself, and now you've broadcast it across the state."

"I get it. Kind of like what you did to me with that newspaper article." Taylor leaned against the side of his truck, apparently not caring whether or not the dried mud rubbed off on him.

"It's not the same thing at all," she said. "The newspaper article was part of my job, a way to publicize the team. What you did tonight—there's no excuse for that."

"You know what I think, Rebecca? I think all your public-relations work and all your picture taking is just a way for you to put the spotlight on someone else, but never on yourself. You hide behind that camera of yours."

"I never hide from anything. I had to take a lot of risks to build my own business. And I've had to sell my skills to my clients—*that's* not hiding. Everything in my life was going just fine, until..." She couldn't go on, not around Taylor. She yanked open her car door, but Taylor stopped her from sliding behind the wheel.

"Tell me about it," he said. "Tell me about your life, and what's happened to it."

"Why? So you can broadcast my problems to the whole world via satellite?" She closed her car door and slumped back against it. "I've worked so hard to build up my career. Twelve-hour days, putting every cent I could into the business—and I've loved it. I've loved it, and having a two-seater sports car and all the independence in the world! Sure, I kept telling myself that someday I'd meet someone special and have a family, but there wasn't any rush. Why should there be a rush?'' She frowned at Taylor. "Well, there shouldn't be a rush. But all of a sudden I'm buying rocking horses and stuffed bears, and there doesn't seem to be a thing I can do about it. You think I want to feel this way? It's all supposed to be so different!'' She took a deep breath, and tried to sound calm and logical when she went on.

"I'll tell you how it's supposed to be, Taylor. You're supposed to be going along just fine, enjoying your career, your independence. And then you meet a man. Not someone you were actually looking for—after all, you're supposed to be having too much fun with your life to worry about a man being around. But you meet him, anyway, and something special happens. Something magical. Now you've met him, you can't live without him. And that's when you start wanting kids—his kids. You want to see what a kid will look like with his smile or his eyes. You're not supposed to get the order all reversed. You're not supposed to dream about the kids before the man comes along, and you're sure not supposed to buy the rocking horse before you even have the baby!''

There. She was done. She'd let all her frustration spill out. It was a relief in a way. She tapped her car keys against her palm, waiting to see what Taylor would make of her confession.

"Seems to me you're being too idealistic," he said doubtfully. "Okay, that's the way you'd like things to be, and it sounds good to you. But maybe you have to revise your expectations."

Beck shook her head. "Didn't you listen to those callers, McCoy? Desperate widowers, and men who practically offered to do gene splicing before they even met me! That's what happens when you get everything out of order. When you don't put romance first, it's just hopeless."

"There's only one problem," he said. "Things are already out of order for you. You want kids, and you want them bad."

"It's like I told you. I didn't ask to feel this way. I don't *want* to feel this way. What on earth am I going to do?"

Taylor didn't have an answer for that. Maybe nobody did. Somehow Beck's life had gotten out of whack, and she didn't have a single idea what to do about it.

CHAPTER FOUR

BECK MOVED down the aisle of the plane, trying to be as unobtrusive as possible as she snapped a photo here and there. She wanted candid shots of team members as they relaxed on this flight to Oklahoma. Tomorrow they would be facing a rival club in a game crucial to making the playoffs, but for now the Roadrunners could forget the pressure a bit. Beck captured four ball players intent on a game of poker, then edged forward to snap the left fielder snoring contentedly with his feet up, the second baseman deep into a mystery novel—and then she made the mistake of swiveling her camera in Taylor McCoy's direction.

"Rebecca," he greeted her with suspicious heartiness, "I was just talking about you. In fact, I was just telling Alan here that he ought to meet you." Taylor stood up and motioned toward the man in the seat beside him. "Beck, this is Alan Silva. Alan's a lawyer from Albuquerque. He's traveling to Oklahoma City to visit his brother. Have a seat, Beck, have a seat. Stay and talk to Alan awhile."

Taylor was being overly officious. Before Beck knew it, he prodded her down into the seat he'd just vacated. Her camera dangling from the strap at her neck, she turned automatically to give this Alan Silva a handshake. But Alan's pleasant face barely registered with her; she was too busy wondering exactly what Taylor McCoy was up to. After that embarrassing talk show at KQIZ Radio two weeks ago, she didn't trust him at all.

Taylor settled down in a seat across the aisle and smiled magnanimously at Beck. "I think you'll find that you and Alan have a lot in common. He was just telling me how much he's looking forward to seeing his nieces and nephews. Alan sure likes kids, don't you, Alan?"

Now it was very clear what Taylor was up to. Beck glared at him, but he just kept smiling. She turned to Alan, wanting to apologize, but the man didn't seem to find anything amiss. Perhaps Taylor had shown a little self-restraint and hadn't gone into too much detail about Beck's "baby hunger."

"Yes, I do like children," Alan said easily. "I haven't seen my brother's kids for a couple of years now, and I have a lot of catching up to do. It's easy to lose touch with family, isn't it?"

"Yes, it is," Beck murmured. She spent a few moments chatting with Alan, who seemed a likable enough fellow. But it was difficult maintaining a polite conversation with him while sending a disapproving stare across the aisle toward Taylor. So now Taylor had decided to play matchmaker for her! She couldn't wait to get him alone and tell him exactly what she thought of *that*.

When the conversation between Beck and Alan threatened to die away, Taylor jumped right in. "Alan, Beck owns her own public-relations firm. She's very good at her job. Maybe you could use her services sometime."

Beck gazed sourly at Taylor. What do you know—he was actually complimenting her on her job, after all his complaints about it.

"Go ahead, Beck," he urged, leaning across the aisle. "Give Alan your card. Better write your home phone on it, just in case he wants to reach you there."

Reluctantly Beck took one of her cards from her camera bag and handed it to Alan.

"That's my business phone," she said dryly. "If you ever do need any public-relations work, please don't hesitate to call me, Mr. Silva."

"Er...fine," Alan said, taking the card and beginning to look just a little uncomfortable. Beck felt sorry for the poor man. He was a perfectly nice normal person on the way to visit his brother, and he'd had the misfortune to sit next to Taylor McCoy, budding marriage broker. Any minute now Taylor was probably going to suggest outright that Alan set the date for a nice little Southwestern wedding. Instead, Taylor pumped the man for information about the extent of his law practice, his annual income—and whether or not he owned a family-size car.

Beck glanced from one man to the other. Alan Silva was attractive in his own way. But Taylor...well, Taylor had something special—he had a passion that could come only from living and breathing baseball. All Beck had to do was look at him, and she could start to imagine the fresh rich grass of a playing field, could almost hear the powerful smack of wood against leather as the bat hit the ball. Taylor gave off an aura of excitement. It was as simple as that. And now that she'd started to hang around him a little, other men didn't quite measure up. It wasn't that Beck wanted

Taylor McCoy, but after knowing him it was hard to imagine settling for anything less....

Beck tried to sit back and relax, but the throbbing of the plane engines seemed to echo her own inner disquiet. Here she was, cataloging Taylor's virtues as if he were a fine wine that had corrupted her palate for other vintages. And yet she'd known him barely a few weeks.

Standing abruptly, Beck almost bumped her head on the luggage compartment above. Clutching her camera bag, she turned toward Alan Silva.

"It was a pleasure meeting you, and I hope you have a good visit with your brother's family. But you'll have to excuse me—I'm on the job right now. I need to take some more publicity photos."

Alan offered a few polite inanities in return. She could tell he wasn't particularly shaken up to see her go, but Taylor acted concerned.

"You don't have to work so hard, Beck. We were just getting started here. I thought—"

"Exactly *what* did you think?" she said more acidly than she'd intended.

Taylor leaned closer to Beck, so that only she could hear what he was saying. "I saw an opportunity to help you with your dilemma. Naturally I had to take advantage of it."

"Naturally."

"This is the way I look at it, Rebecca. You've got a problem—one doozy of a problem. Yet you're not making enough effort on your own behalf. That's your biggest mistake right there. So of course somebody like me has to step in and...encourage things. Makes sense, doesn't it?"

Beck was tempted to snap a photo of the smug expression on Taylor's face. "The only real problem I have is your interference," she muttered. "Got it?"

He just kept on smiling, apparently quite satisfied with himself. "Someone has to take charge of things, Rebecca. If you're not going to do it, then why not me?"

"Keep your nose out of my personal life," she blurted much too loudly. Alan Silva chose this moment to pick up an airline magazine and disappear firmly behind it.

IT WASN'T UNTIL LATE that night that Beck finally had a free minute to herself. The game had been a grueling one for the team. The dry climate of New Mexico meant that the Roadrunners weren't at their best playing in more humid weather, and it had taken everything they had to win by two runs. Up in the comfort of the stands it wasn't possible to see how much exertion was required by the players; baseball was a deceptively casual game. But tonight Beck had been near the Roadrunners' dugout with her camera, and she'd seen the intensity and concentration of the players as they'd struggled to win.

She'd also seen how Taylor had encouraged and goaded each of his players toward their hard-won victory. He didn't sit still during a game, that was for sure. He paced ceaselessly, observing the game from different angles, sending signals to his players in a graceful yet brusque sign language all his own: a finger tipped to his cap, a fist thumped against his chest, a hand brushed emphatically down his arm or clapped to his elbow. Beck had been able to sense the energy coiled in him. At one point she'd been convinced he was about to sprint out onto the field, grab a bat and take a shot at a home run himself. She'd known that was what he wanted to do, anyway.

Now the game was over and Beck was sitting in the hotel coffee shop, a cup of decaf growing cold in front of her. She had her notebook open and was concentrating on how to promote the team's road games. There had to be a way, although even the most diehard fans couldn't always afford to follow the Roadrunners out of town. She tapped her pen against her notepad, wondering if she could get one of the local television stations in Albuquerque to cover the out-of-town games. Or perhaps she could shoot videos of the road games to sell later at the souvenir stand in Albuquerque. Yes, that might do....

Glancing up, she saw Taylor come into the coffee shop with a few of his players. He looked toward her, tipping his cap the way he did when he was signaling the man on first to steal second. Beck merely raised her eyebrows in a skeptical response. She watched as Taylor sat down with his players, then she recapped her pen and stuffed her notepad into her camera bag. She didn't really need to work anymore today. Overall, her promotion strategies were going well. Attendance was up at the home games, spurred in large part by interest in the Roadrunners' new manager—Taylor McCoy. And thanks to tonight's game, the team was still headed straight for the league playoffs. Beck could surely go up to her room and sleep with the peaceful knowledge that things were progressing nicely.

Everything was progressing nicely, of course, but her personal life. That area left quite a bit to be desired. At the game, simply of its own volition, her camera had sought out children in the stands: a four-year-old dragging along a baseball mitt almost bigger than he was, a freckled little girl jumping up and down the steps in a race with her brother, a pair of sisters wearing identical baseball caps and team T-shirts. Why did she have to see children absolutely *everywhere* she went?

She stood up and headed for the door. Taylor stood up and headed for the door at the same time. She quickened her pace; he sped up a little, too, and intercepted her.

"Hello, Beck. Join me for a cup of coffee?"

"Right. I suppose you want to introduce me to the waiter."

"No way—he's not your type. Besides, he's already married, with three kids."

Beck looked at him hard, not putting it past him actually to check out the marital status of every male in her vicinity.

"I just had coffee, Taylor."

"You didn't have any with me, though." He ushered her to another table in a secluded corner. A few moments later they were seated with two steaming mugs in front of them. Taylor removed his cap and hung it from the back of his chair. "Why'd you take off in such a hurry after I introduced you to Alan Silva? The guy was prime father material if ever I saw it."

Beck grimaced. "Give it a rest, will you? Besides, he wasn't even interested in me. Anybody could see that."

"Why wouldn't he be interested?" Taylor regarded her speculatively. "Yep, you're a good-looking woman. Right height, hair's the right color. You're in fair shape, too. Bet you could run a decent forty if you had to. What more could Alan Silva want?"

Beck hardly felt flattered. Taylor was talking about her as if sizing up a recruit for spring training. "Maybe Alan would be more impressed with me if I could do a hundred push-ups," she remarked.

"You're still waiting for romance to strike out of the blue, I take it. But you have to meet somebody first. Do you go anywhere you could actually meet a new guy, Beck?"

"I meet plenty of people through my work."

"I hear woodworking classes are a good place to look. Or maybe an auto-mechanics class. Or ball-room dancing."

Beck sighed. "I don't want to go out looking for a man! I want my old life back. No vague yearnings, no man problems."

Taylor stirred a generous spoonful of sugar into his coffee. "You're telling me there were no guys in your old life, after all?"

Beck stirred cream into her own coffee a bit too vigorously. "Listen, Taylor, I've dated plenty. That's not the problem. It's just that . . . it never seemed to matter much before if a relationship didn't work out. I've always had so much else in my life." She gazed down into her coffee as if seeing all the years when she'd been so busy and contented. For some reason it seemed important to make Taylor see those years, too.

"It's funny," she murmured. "I started out study-ing photography in college. I'd never thought about public relations work at all. But I had a boyfriend who played in a bluegrass band, and I was always taking pictures of them. My photos turned into publicity shots, I helped the band line up a few gigs, and that was the beginning of my career. I've had a wonderful time ever since."

She should have known better than to share the story with Taylor. He picked up on all the wrong details.

"So what happened to the boyfriend?" he asked. "The two of you couldn't mix business with pleasure?"

Beck hesitated. "Mitch and I were good friends. It just turned out that dating wasn't right for us. He's married now—quite happily, in fact. A couple of times a year he and his wife throw a party, get the band together to perform, and I take pictures for old times' sake."

Taylor nodded solemnly. "Let me guess. Mitch and spouse have several kids . . . and you can't help thinking those kids could've been yours."

"That's not the way it is at all! I'm pleased for Mitch and his wife, and yes, their children. But I was never in love with him."

Taylor didn't seem to hear a word. "Your problem is more serious than I thought, Rebecca. Sounds like you're prone to let opportunity slip you by. First Mitch, now Alan Silva. I sense a pattern here."

Beck gripped her mug. "Okay, Taylor. I think you've had enough fun. But *I'm* not the one with the real problem. It's you. You're a confirmed bachelor—and according to half the women in New Mexico, that means you're seriously in need of a cure."

Taylor didn't look perturbed. "Afraid there is no cure. It's a terminal case of bachelorhood. See, this is the difference between you and me, Beck. I'm happy without a wife or kids, and I aim to keep it that way. But you're itching for a family. You just don't know how to take the first step."

"And I'm fortunate enough to have you around to help." Beck pulled out her notebook again. In spite of the way Taylor was needling her, she suddenly felt quite inspired. This conversation had given her an excellent idea, and she couldn't wait to get it down on paper. She smiled a little to herself as she jotted down notes.

"What's so funny?" Taylor asked, swigging coffee.

"Nothing you should worry about right now. But let me tell you something. Public relations is definitely the right field for me. Boy, am I in the right job." She couldn't help smiling again.

Taylor gave her a suspicious glance. "I don't like that look on your face. I've seen it before. First day we met, you were wearing that look. Next thing I knew, I ended up in the newspapers."

"Oh, this time it's going to be much better than that, Taylor. Wait and see!"

THE STADIUM in Albuquerque was crowded, the fans restless for the game to begin. But the game couldn't begin, not as long as Taylor McCoy stood at home plate with his arms crossed, frowning at Beck. She'd never seen him look this ominous before. Really, that scowl of his was daunting, but she wasn't about to back down. It was much too late for that, anyway. She stood on the other side of the plate and gazed at him calmly.

"We've already been through all this, Taylor. You agreed to the plan. What good will second thoughts do you now?"

"Dammit, Rebecca, you and Alma Latham cornered me into this thing. I never once agreed to it. Not voluntarily, anyway."

"Well, yes, it does help when the owner of the team is on your side," Beck conceded. "Mrs. Latham thinks this is my best idea yet." Beck gestured up at the stands. "Look at all those people! The first sellout crowd of the season."

"That's my point," Taylor muttered. "Sure, we sold out, but ninety percent of the people up there are *women.*"

"And they're all here because of you," Beck said with satisfaction. "Thousands of women here because they have a chance to personally cure you of bachelorhood. Did I come up with a great idea or what?"

Taylor groaned, took off his cap and then slapped it back on again. His displeasure seemed to have reached such proportions he could no longer express it in mere words. Beck thought back over the past week and the advertising campaign she'd mounted in the newspapers, on the radio and on television. All of Beck's advertisements had proclaimed that Saturday was Ladies Day at the ball park. A special contest would be held, the lucky winner to be treated to a date with handsome, confirmed bachelor Taylor McCoy. Yes, the lucky winner would have an entire evening in which to try curing Taylor of his bachelorhood.

"I guess you still don't understand," Beck told him now. "You're so adamant about being single you've thrown out an irresistible challenge to the female population. You've built a wall around yourself that women are just dying to climb. Haven't you ever experienced something similar yourself? Somebody tells you you can't do something, so of course you have to try, just to see if you can—"

"Enough," Taylor said, rubbing his shoulder. "I swear I can feel ten thousand pairs of female eyes boring into me. It's not a feeling I like, Rebecca."

"It's too bad you can't enjoy the moment. A sell-out crowd, all here to see your team play."

Nothing she said seemed to reassure Taylor. He shoved up the sleeves of his jersey. "Just remember, Rebecca, what goes around comes around."

Beck wondered if this meant Taylor was going to show up on her doorstep some day with ten thousand potential fathers in tow. That *was* an appalling thought, and for the first time she felt a twinge of sympathy for Taylor.

"Look at it this way," she said. "In a short while we'll have the contestants narrowed down to a handful of women, and it'll be only one woman in the end. The sooner you get started with this game, the sooner it'll all be over."

Taylor pulled his cap low over his forehead. "Play ball," he muttered to Beck in a tone of deep disgust, and then he strode away. Organ music crescendoed cheerfully, and cries of "*Pop*corn! *Pea*nuts!" came from the vendors in the stands.

Beck watched Taylor until he reached the Roadrunners' dugout. "Play ball," she echoed under her breath, and then she hurried to make last-minute preparations for her contest. Something told her this would be a day she'd remember for a long time.

During the seventh-inning stretch, five ticket numbers were chosen at random and read over the loudspeaker. A few moments later, the possessors of the lucky tickets jogged out onto the playing field: five women who all had a chance at Taylor McCoy. But now came the difficult part. The real winner would be the woman who could take a bat and hit the ball the farthest.

The first contestant positioned herself at home plate. She warmed up, swinging the bat vigorously with one hand. She looked like she knew what she was doing, but when the Roadrunners' pitcher lobbed the ball her way, she missed completely. Second pitch ... strike two! Third pitch ... the bat connected, and the ball went flying impressively far into the outfield. A cheer went up from the crowd, and the next contestant came to bat.

Beck had been snapping photographs, but now she noticed that Taylor was sending suspicious-looking signals to his pitcher. Three taps to the chest, a hand slapped to his shoulder, two fingers to his cap ... She strode over to him.

"Taylor, you'd better not try to sabotage this contest. No fastballs!"

"Come on, is this supposed to be a fair competition or what? I have the same rules for women as for men. My pitcher throws a strike, no matter who's up to bat— Damn!" He watched as the bat made contact with the ball, and contestant number two waved a triumphant fist in the air. This time the ball went even farther than before.

Taylor didn't appear happy, but already the third contestant was up. She gripped the bat, looking mean and ready. The pitcher went through his ballet of motion: arms held loosely, ball hidden in his glove, then one leg rising fluently into the air, arm rotating back, the ball flowing from his hand...

"Striiike one!" yelled the umpire.

The woman at the plate tapped her bat against the ground and positioned herself once again. She looked more determined than ever. But when she took a swing at the ball, she missed by a wide margin.

"Striiike two!"

One more chance. The woman hunched over the plate, eyes narrowed at the pitcher.

"Striiike three! You're out!"

Apparently this was too much for the woman. She flung down her bat and confronted the umpire. She went nose to nose with him, arguing about the call. The crowd loved it—and as far as Beck was concerned, it was a photographer's dream. She adjusted her lens just in time to capture the umpire's face turning fire-engine red. He lifted his arm and jabbed a finger toward the exit gate.

"You're *outta* here!" he hollered.

The woman promptly scuffed her feet over the ground, kicking red earth on the umpire's shoes. The umpire waved both arms now, his cheeks puffed in outrage. The woman simply stepped closer to him and kicked more dirt.

Beck quickly snapped another picture or two, then glanced at Taylor. "Too bad that lady struck out," she observed. "I think she could've been perfect for you. After all, the two of you share the same tactics when it comes to umpires."

"There has to be justice in this world," Taylor muttered. "Somehow, someday, you'll be sorry you ever put me through this, Rebecca."

The next two contestants both got hits, one of them becoming the undisputed winner of the day: a very pretty blonde who ran over to Taylor, pumped his hand excitedly, and then ran over to shake hands with the pitcher. She even went to shake hands with the umpire. Taylor watched all this handshaking with interest.

"Say, Rebecca, this idea of yours might not be so bad, after all. Maybe I've been too close-minded about the whole thing."

She glanced at him sharply. "Why the sudden about-face?"

"I'm trying to look at it in a new way, for your sake. What's so bad about it, after all? A long leisurely evening spent in the company of a beautiful woman. What guy in his right mind is going to turn that down?"

Beck swiveled and focused her zoom on the blonde. Okay, the woman was pretty, but beautiful? That seemed to be overstating the case.

"Don't you agree with me, Beck?" Taylor prodded. "That was your intention, anyway—to have me spend the evening with a beautiful woman. Hey, I'm almost starting to feel grateful." Taylor began to look comfortable and relaxed, pushing his cap back on his forehead.

Beck popped a new roll of film into her camera and cranked it into place. This *was* what she'd wanted from Taylor all along—some cooperation....

But she couldn't prevent a trifling little doubt from surfacing. Maybe, just maybe, her contest to raffle off Taylor McCoy wasn't the best idea she'd ever had, after all.

CHAPTER FIVE

TAYLOR'S NEW COOPERATIVE spirit did not extend in all directions. In fact, on some points he was downright intractable. After the game was over—another satisfying win by the Roadrunners—Beck met Taylor outside the team's locker room. He'd changed from his uniform into dark trousers and the tan jacket that complemented his coloring so well. Beck tried not to be distracted by the trim fit of his jacket or by the fresh scent of his cologne.

"You'd better hurry," she said. "I have a limousine waiting for you and Danielle. That's her name, by the way, Danielle Meyers. I have a wonderful time planned for the two of you. A drive to the foothills and then you'll take the tram up to Sandia Crest. You'll share an elegant dinner overlooking the—"

"No limo. No fancy restaurant. We'll be doing this my way." Taylor strode down the concourse, and Beck had to rush to catch up.

"Hold on. This is a publicity event. I have it all arranged, and I'm going along to take pictures. I'll remain in the background, of course, but all the same..."

He stopped to gaze at her. "You're coming, too? I didn't know I was going on a date with two women at the same time. That's an interesting idea."

"You're not going on a date with *me*, for goodness' sake. I'll merely be documenting the, uh, event. Technically you're not even going on a real date with Danielle. It's publicity for the team, and—"

"I wouldn't want to be guilty of false advertising. If we're going to tell the public I went on a date, I'll have to make it a real date. That means no photographs, Beck. No limousine, either." He went on down the concourse, Beck hurrying once again to keep pace with him.

"I've worked too hard to pull this thing off. I'm coming along as your publicist."

"Fine. But your camera's not allowed. I'll have enough to worry about, dating two women at the same time and all."

"I told you. This isn't a date with me!" She was starting to holler almost as loud as the umpire had, and a few fans still straggling out of the stands looked at her. She clamped her mouth shut until she could trust herself to go on in a more reasoned tone.

"Okay, Taylor," she continued at last. "Exactly what are your plans for the evening? Maybe we can compromise a little and still make this something people will want to read about."

"Guess you'll just have to come along for the ride and find out that way. Let's get started. We're going to have fun tonight, aren't we, Beck? The three of us."

She managed to restrain herself from making several belligerent comments. Outside, Danielle Meyers was waiting beside a lovely white stretch limousine.

"I'm sorry, Danielle, but we have a little change of plans. Mr. McCoy would prefer a more . . . informal outing."

"I don't mind," Danielle said promptly. "Whatever Taylor wants to do is okay with me." She smiled at him. It was clear that Danielle had good teeth. Well, fine. There were plenty of cute blondes around who made regular visits to the dentist. Taylor had no reason to look so pleased at the moment.

Skirting the limo, Taylor led both women over to his big mud-spattered truck and opened the door for them. Here Beck protested.

"Taylor, this isn't exactly the type of vehicle I had in mind. It seems like we could reach a medium somewhere between a limousine and a fifty-year-old pickup."

"Oh, I don't mind," said Danielle. "I love old trucks, Taylor."

"Is that so." Taylor gave Beck a meaningful glance. "You heard it right here, Rebecca. Danielle doesn't mind. She likes old trucks."

Beck took a deep breath, reminding herself that a good publicist knew how to exercise restraint when dealing with clients. She lifted her camera.

"All right, Danielle. Move over a little to the left, please. I want a shot of you getting in the—"

"No camera," Taylor said. "Remember?"

It was only with a great effort of will that Beck kept her finger from pressing the shutter. She stared at Taylor, and he stared right back. After a long moment, she screwed on her lens cap.

"Okay, okay," she grumbled. "No photos. But I can't very well leave my camera in the street. I'll have to bring it with me."

"Don't try sneaking any pictures," he warned.

"You've made your point. Can we just get on with this darn—I mean, this enjoyable evening we have ahead of us?"

Danielle ended up sandwiched between Beck and Taylor in the truck. The three of them jounced out of the parking lot. It seemed to Beck that Danielle was cozying up a bit much to Taylor. Beck scooted closer to the door.

"I don't want you to feel cramped, Danielle. There's plenty of room."

"I don't mind," Danielle said instantly, and she remained snugly pressed against Taylor. Beck wondered if there was anything Danielle *would* mind where Taylor McCoy was concerned.

Taylor drove along the streets of Albuquerque, eventually heading out Rio Grande Boulevard. This was one of Beck's favorite parts of town, green fields and adobe houses spread out on either side. The setting sun gave everything a golden cast, mellow light drifting down hazily through the leaves of the cottonwoods. Taylor and Danielle seemed to be enjoying the scenery, too, apparently neither one of them feeling the need for conversation. Beck suspected she was the only one who found the silence uncomfortable. She fished her notebook out of her bag.

"So, Danielle," she said. "Tell us a little about yourself. What do you do for a living?"

"I'm a systems analyst. My specialty is helping companies downsize from mainframes to personal-computer networks. Networking is the only way to go these days, you know."

"Absolutely," said Taylor. "I agree." He glanced over at Beck, who was industriously jotting down notes. So, Danielle Meyers was not only pretty, she was smart, too.

"Tell us more about yourself, Danielle," Taylor said, taking up where Beck had left off. "What do you like to do in your spare time?"

"I waterski whenever I get a chance. Let's see . . . I like racquetball and swimming. Hiking in the mountains, too."

"An athlete," Taylor remarked. "I could tell it right off, the way you hit that ball. Impressive."

Beck shut her notebook. She figured she'd recorded enough of this evening for a while.

By now the road was winding through an even more rural setting. Horses grazed in the pastures, and a peacock perched on a crumbling adobe wall, vivid plumage spread for show. Taylor pulled over into the dirt parking lot of a low-slung building with a sagging front porch. Cora's Kitchen read a faded sign.

"Best Greek food in the Southwest," Taylor announced. "Hope you like Greek food, Danielle."

"I love it."

Of course. What else could the woman be expected to say? She'd probably agree to eat barley grass, as long as she could do it in Taylor's company. Beck clambered down from the truck, deciding that some females were altogether too compliant.

The inside of Cora's Kitchen wasn't much more fashionable than the outside: a few booths against the walls, veneered tables scattered over the uneven floor. Taylor seated Danielle at one of the tables, then pulled out a chair for Beck. Originally she'd planned to sit discreetly at another table, allowing Taylor and his "date" at least a semblance of privacy while she snapped photos from afar. But Taylor seemed determined to change the rules of the game. She sat down unabashedly.

Perhaps Beck was cynical about Cora's Kitchen, but when the food came, she started to feel more kindly toward the place. It was definitely a feast: steaming onion stew, spinach pie with feta cheese and flaky layers of phyllo, stuffed grape leaves plump with minty rice and beef.

The good food seemed to loosen Danielle's tongue. She smiled at Taylor over a glass of ouzo. "You know, I've been hearing all these rumors about you, and I wonder if they can possibly be true. Are you really as confirmed a bachelor as they say?"

He took his time answering, gazing at Beck all the while. "It's what my publicist says about me," he murmured finally. "So it must be the truth."

By this time Danielle seemed rather impatient with Beck's presence. She brought her chair closer to Taylor's, turning away from Beck.

"Tell me what *you* say about yourself," she urged. "I'm not interested in anybody's opinion but yours."

Taylor took a sip of his own drink, then raised his glass in a mock toast to Beck. "Have to admit I am a confirmed bachelor. Those stories in the newspaper aren't exaggerated."

Danielle propped her chin on her hand. "It's still a mystery. What's made you this way?"

"Any number of things," Taylor said, still gazing at Beck. "It's a complicated matter, this business of being a bachelor."

Beck flipped to a new page in her ever-ready notebook. This was a most interesting conversation: Danielle asking Taylor questions, Taylor answering the questions by addressing Beck. It was a new angle on the proverbial triangle, that was certain.

"Tell me just one reason you're a bachelor," Danielle persisted, her voice growing a little husky.

"A baseball career isn't conducive to romance," Taylor said, leaning over as if to make sure Beck was writing all this down. "You're on the road too much, and when you *are* in town, you gotta be out at the ball park practicing. It's the kind of life-style that would drive most women nuts. I've seen a lot of marriages break up in my time. Wouldn't want that to happen to me."

Danielle twisted a strand of her long silky hair around her finger. "Some women might not mind a setup like that. It could be ideal. You have a man around at certain times, but when he leaves you can go back to your own schedule."

"The best-of-both-worlds theory," Taylor said. "Sorry, I've heard that one before. Never works out— women always want more, no matter what they say in the beginning."

"All a ball player needs is a woman with her own interests, her own career," Danielle said confidently.

"Yeah, but what about when the kids come along?" Taylor asked. "You tell me any woman wants a husband who's an absentee father?"

Danielle didn't seem to have an answer to that one, and Beck stepped into the breach.

"So don't get married, Taylor. Nobody's twisting your arm."

Danielle frowned. "Um . . . I believe I'll make a little trip to the powder room. Why don't you come with me, Rebecca?"

"I'm fine. I'll just stay here with Taylor and wait for you."

"Rebecca, I really think you need a visit to the powder room, too."

Deciding this was more than a hint, Beck pushed back her chair and obligingly traipsed after Danielle. She glanced over her shoulder and saw Taylor looking at her with amusement. What did he find so entertaining, anyway?

The rest-room facilities at Cora's Kitchen hardly qualified as a powder room. The mirror over the chipped sinks was cloudy and had a jagged crack down the middle, but Danielle peered into it, anyway, checking her lipstick and fluffing her hair.

"Rebecca, let's be straight with each other. You're starting to cramp my style. Why don't you tell Taylor you have a headache or something and ask him to drop you off at your house? Then I can concentrate on him a little better."

For some reason Beck wasn't in the mood to be amenable. "Sorry, Danielle. This is a publicity event to promote the Roadrunners, and I have to document it thoroughly." Beck peered into the foggy mirror, too, wondering if she ought to engage in some feminine primping of her own. But her short hair never required much in the way of combing, and actually looked its best when tousled a little. She merely waited while Danielle fiddled with her pretty blond tresses.

"You still have plenty of time to cure Taylor of bachelorhood," Beck remarked. "I won't get in your way."

"You told him he should be *happy* as a bachelor. How's that supposed to help me?"

"From now on I'll try to keep my opinions to myself. It won't be easy, but I'll do it, for the sake of fairness."

Danielle turned away from the mirror. "Let me put this another way, Rebecca. Buzz off!"

These were fighting words, indeed, and Beck was equal to the challenge. "Afraid it can't be done, Danielle. I'm Taylor's publicist, remember?"

"You'll hardly let me forget," Danielle said icily, exiting the ladies' room and striding back toward Taylor. As Beck followed once again, she was well aware how absurd this situation had become. Anyone would think she and Danielle were rivals vying for Taylor's attention. Beck had more pride than that, surely; for a moment she was almost tempted to leave Danielle alone with the man, after all. But then she saw that Taylor still wore a look of quiet amusement. Perhaps he was enjoying the fact that this outing wasn't going according to Beck's plans. Well, she'd see the whole thing through; nothing else for it. She sat down at the table and, in spite of Danielle's disapproving glare, ate her entire dessert of anisette cookies.

Evening was deepening into night when the three of them emerged from the restaurant. Taylor swung open the door of his truck.

"Pile in," he said genially. "Next we're going to indulge in one of my favorite pastimes."

"I'm sure it'll be wonderful," Danielle said. "I don't care where you take us—I mean, I don't care where you take *me*."

Beck wondered what he had in mind. A movie or dancing? Miniature golf, even? But Taylor surprised her. He simply drove to the river, pulling onto the sandy bank and cutting the engine. The water of the Rio Grande spread out in front of them, glimmering in the dusk. Taylor sat and gazed through the windshield, his expression abstracted now. Beck had seen that look come over his face at odd moments before, as if he was remembering something both distressful and pleasurable at the same time. She was content to sit back and let him go on remembering. This time it was Danielle who seemed to find the silence uncomfortable.

"Let's walk along the river," she said. "There's just not a whole lot of...privacy in this truck."

Taylor stirred. "Sure," he said, still abstracted. "We'll walk. But sometimes I like to come out here and sit and enjoy the view."

"Oh, the view would be wonderful if it weren't so *crowded*." Danielle gazed pointedly at Beck, but to no avail. When Taylor and Danielle climbed down to the water's edge, Beck made sure to stay right beside them.

"We're the Three Musketeers, after all," Beck muttered under her breath, stopping to slip off her shoes.

"What was that?" Danielle said.

"Nothing you want to hear." Beck waded into the water, relishing its coolness. Two wild ducks skimmed across to the far shore, apparently resenting Beck's presence as much as Danielle did.

After a moment Danielle took hold of Taylor's hand and pulled him ahead. "I want to talk to you some more about this bachelor thing. Doesn't it bother you that someday you'll be lonely? And that maybe someday you'll realize you met the right woman, but you let her slip away from you? Wouldn't that be terrible?" Danielle's voice had gone husky again. It was certainly an encouraging combination for romance: a man and a woman strolling hand in hand along the water's edge at rose-colored twilight discussing matters of the heart. Beck supposed she wasn't contributing to the atmosphere by splashing alongside the potential lovebirds. Taylor glanced over Danielle's head, once again addressing himself to Beck.

"I don't happen to believe there *is* a right woman out there for me. Another part of being a ball player— especially when you've been in the majors—is having women hang around you only because you're some kind of celebrity. That doesn't go very deep."

"Taylor," Danielle said, "I want to get to know you better—the real you, that is. If we had some time to ourselves, maybe you could get to know me, too."

Beck splashed a little louder. "Don't mind me. You two just go ahead and get to know each other better. Forget I'm even here."

Danielle pulled Taylor along faster. "Like I was saying—what are you really like, Taylor, underneath the baseball facade?"

"Baseball's no facade. It's my life. It *was* my life." Again the sense of pain lurked underneath his words. He extracted his fingers from Danielle's grasp and stuffed both hands into his trouser pockets. "Let's not talk about me, Danielle. Let's talk about you, instead. What else do you like to do in your spare time besides hike and play racquetball?"

Danielle wasn't dense; clearly she recognized the brush-off Taylor was giving her. She answered desultorily that she liked to knit. The conversation lagged after this, and Beck dropped back to the rear, wading more quietly. Maybe she ought to give Danielle a chance with Taylor, after all. But Taylor wasn't the best company himself tonight, retreating into his earlier abstraction. A few moments later they all turned around and headed for the truck. The date with Taylor was officially over.

Taylor took Danielle home first. Beck forced herself to remain in the truck while he walked Danielle to her front door. The two of them stood on the porch, Danielle talking in a low murmur while Taylor listened politely. Beck watched them, lifting one of her damp feet to brush off the sand. Danielle glanced toward the truck in the driveway, and Beck waved cheerfully through the open window. Apparently this simple gesture galvanized Danielle into action. She turned back to Taylor, grabbed him by the shoulders and gave him a full-fledged kiss.

The kiss seemed to go on for an excessively long time, and Beck was tempted to honk the horn to disrupt it. When at last it was over, Danielle disappeared into her house with a show of reluctance, and Taylor came strolling back to the truck. He climbed in without saying a word, and followed Beck's directions to her apartment complex. When he pulled into the parking lot, she could no longer contain herself.

"You seemed to enjoy that kiss," she remarked as casually as possible. "Maybe tonight was a success, after all."

The truck rolled into the space beside her little sports coupe. "If that's your criterion for success— sure."

Beck didn't find this answer satisfactory in the least. "Of course, it's going to be a little difficult describing this evening for the newspapers. I suppose I'll concentrate on how good the food was at Cora's Kitchen."

Taylor stared out the windshield. "Listen, Rebecca, this whole damn thing has gone far enough. I don't need any more women trying to cure me of being a bachelor!"

"I should think you'd look forward to being cured by someone like Danielle. She's intelligent, peppy..."

"She's not my type," Taylor grumbled.

Beck felt a sense of relief she didn't want to analyze too closely. "Better luck next time, then. Because I can't stop things now. This campaign has taken on a life of its own. You'll have your pick of women who want to cure you for a long time to come."

He swore and thumped his hand against the steering wheel. "It was bad enough in the majors. Women hanging around the locker room, waiting for any ball player who happened to step out. You know something, Beck? It feels pretty flattering—for a while. You get caught up in all the damn publicity, the admiration. You want more of it. And then, just like that, it's over. You get an injury, you can't play the way you did, and before you know it they've given your locker to somebody else. You're out of the show."

Taylor didn't speak for a long time after that. He just sat in the truck, and Beck sat beside him, wishing she didn't feel his pain. It was too raw, like a wound that hadn't healed. At last he went on.

"I didn't miss the publicity. I finally understood that for what it was—a bunch of empty images. And I didn't miss the women hanging around. I finally understood that, too. I realized not one of them wanted me unless I could be a star. What I missed—" He stopped again, but this time Beck finished for him.

"You missed swinging that bat," she said softly. "You missed the chance of hitting the ball out of the park. I know, Taylor."

He moved restlessly. "I can't bring that back," he said, his voice harsh. "My shoulder'll never be what it used to be. My days of being a baseball star are over. So why do I have to contend with more publicity, and more women who only want what's on the surface? Why'd you start it up all over again, Beck?"

She took her camera and twisted the strap around her wrist. "You're a star of a different kind now. You're a natural-born coach, and everyone can sense that—but the type of publicity I believe in isn't superficial. Everything I've been doing is to show people how much you care about the team, how much you inspire the players..."

"The real me?" he said mockingly.

"It *is* the real you. And if women have responded to that, it's perfectly understandable! Any woman would respond—well, almost any woman," she amended. She opened the door of the truck and scrambled out. "Taylor, all in all you were a good sport tonight. But there's one thing you don't need to worry about. We won't be holding any more Ladies' Days at the ball park. No more dates or anything. The whole idea . . . well, I'll admit it did get a little out of hand. I'll be trying other methods in the future. So...good night." She swung her camera bag over her shoulder and went quickly up the walk to her apartment. She didn't want Taylor to come along, but he escorted her, anyway. They stood in front of her apartment, and Beck gazed intently at her keys. Somehow she couldn't seem to remember how to put the right key in the lock of her door. Taylor leaned against the porch railing.

"No good-night kiss?" he asked, his tone quite solemn. She bit her lip. Darn it, she'd like nothing better than to grab him by the shoulders, raise her lips to his and make him completely forget any other goodnight kiss. It took an effort to keep from reaching out to him.

"It's bad enough being the publicist of a confirmed bachelor. Let's not complicate things any more than they already are." Finally she did remember how to get the key in the lock of her door. She escaped from Taylor McCoy—and she escaped from the evening she now considered possibly the worst publicity idea she'd ever had!

CHAPTER SIX

BECK'S WRITE-UP of Taylor's date in the newspapers provoked an unprecedented response. Women seemed charmed that Taylor frequented such quaint establishments as Cora's Kitchen. They thought walks in the dusk by the riverside were indeed romantic. New hope sprang up: surely such a sensitive man as Taylor McCoy couldn't be a true bachelor. Letters poured into the offices of the baseball team, enthusing about Taylor and suggesting all sorts of novel ways he might be converted to the ranks of the married. It was overwhelming.

Beck sat in her own office one afternoon, only a few days after the notorious outing with Danielle. She stared blearily at the piles of mail she'd carted over from the stadium. Her secretary had already made a stab at sorting them, but Beck was trying to read at least some of the letters personally. After all, this was feedback on her campaign for the Roadrunners, and it made good business sense to see how people were responding. She sighed and picked up a card that suggested Taylor obtain a pet—preferably a miniature poodle. "Poodles are known to cultivate the domestic instinct in man," read the card. "Taylor, I raise miniature poodles and would give you a very good price on one of my puppies. Also, I am a healthy, single woman of thirty-five...."

Beck tossed the card aside and picked up the next. And the next...

Half an hour later she buried her head in her hands and moaned. Everybody had a cure for Taylor one way or another. What no one seemed to realize yet was that Taylor McCoy didn't *want* to be cured. These women were simply wasting their time. Beck fished a bright yellow envelope from the pile and scanned the sheet of stationery inside. This letter was not addressed to Taylor. It simply read, "To Whom It May Concern: I would like to state that my very own husband was once a bachelor of the most confirmed sort. It was only after I used my special formula on him that he was transformed into the dear and loving partner I know today..."

Beck rattled the bright yellow page in her hand. Special formula, indeed! She almost sent the letter into the trash can, but a moment later read on.

"My formula is simple, but it must be followed exactly. First, invite Taylor to dinner at your house. Now, this is very important. We are talking a home-cooked meal here. Going out to restaurants is all fine and well, but the way to a man's heart is truly through his stomach. And only a home-cooked meal will do the job properly..."

Beck slapped down the letter. "I was hoping for something more original," she complained. "'The way to a man's heart is through his stomach.' Does anyone believe that anymore?" Apparently someone did believe it—the woman who'd written this letter. Beck had to pick up the yellow sheet of stationery again, just to see what further nonsense might be there.

"You will be serving Taylor a five-course meal. Take careful note: not three courses, not four, not six. Five courses precisely. Course number one will be a light appetizer of oysters and mushrooms. It cannot be ignored that oysters are considered an aphrodisiac. Course number two, a spicy bisque. Course number three, sirloin steak and spring potatoes. Remember, a man always wants to know that he can count on you for his meat and potatoes. Course number four..." Beck refused to make it all the way through to course number five, but she did scan the final paragraph.

"After you have served Taylor and he is pleasantly replete with your cooking, it is time for the final touch. Prop him up with pillows in front of your television and play a romantic old movie on your VCR. For best results, this movie should be *It Happened One Night* with Claudette Colbert and Clark Gable. If you have done your job correctly, by the time the movie is over, Taylor will be completely susceptible to exchanging bachelorhood for married bliss at your side. This formula has worked not only for me, but for several of my friends. I therefore offer you a foolproof guarantee. Please be discreet in sharing this secret, however. I am planning to write a cookbook...."

Beck had read enough. She slapped the silly letter down again and rose to her feet. What was wrong with people? Did some women really need a man that badly?

Taylor McCoy came strolling into her office, baseball cap as usual pushed back from his forehead.

Muttering in disgust, Beck swept all the letters into one big heap and was tempted to light a match to them.

"Hello there, Beck. You seem to be in a good mood today."

"Reading your mail always does that to me. I've just about had it, Taylor! What is this effect you have on women? They want to sell poodles to you, feed you oysters and who knows what else."

He took a chair, straddled it, and rested his arms along the back. "I guess I'll have to remind you—you're the one who started all this. I'm just an innocent bystander."

"Right. Innocent." She looked at him suspiciously. "I can't understand why *you're* in such a good mood. You've been even testier than usual these past few days—and now all of a sudden you're chipper? Doesn't wash, Taylor."

He smiled. "It was the thought of seeing you that cheered me up."

"You saw me yesterday, and that didn't seem to help. You growled the entire time about one thing or another." She glanced at her watch. "Besides, I'm busy right now. I'm running late for an appointment with my clown."

Taylor rubbed his jaw thoughtfully. "I know lawyers charge you for every minute you're late for a meeting, and doctors are liable to bounce you right off their schedule. What exactly are the consequences of standing up a clown?"

Beck stared at Taylor. "Why are you here, anyway? And why do you look so darn cheerful?"

His smile widened. "Maybe it's because I've finally found the answer to your problem, Rebecca. The perfect solution." He took a folded sheet of paper from the pocket of his shirt and handed it over to her. "Just fill this out, and you'll have a man in no time. Quick. Easy. Simple."

Beck snapped open the sheet of paper. "Find-a-Mate Dating Service" it read across the top. "Very funny, Taylor," she said. "Now, do you know any more good jokes?"

"Hey, this is serious. I went to a lot of trouble to track down Find-a-Mate. It's a reputable place. You fill out that information sheet, and they find a match for you. Only you get to look at a videotape of the guy first, just to make sure you want to meet him."

Beck sank down into the chair behind her desk. "A very efficient system all around."

Taylor seemed completely serious. "I've tried introducing you to guys, and it doesn't work. So this is the next step. Find-a-Mate. I like the sound of that. Kinda has a nice ring."

Beck couldn't believe he'd come up with such an unromantic idea. She tossed the form onto her pile of letters. "Forget it, Taylor. No chance."

"Come on, admit it. This baby hunger thing still has you in a pickle."

Beck didn't exactly care for his choice of words, but it was true. She thought about kids all the time. In fact, it seemed as if she'd been thinking about them more and more ever since meeting Taylor.

"I figure what I need to do is work with kids. Join some kind of volunteer organization. That would take care of this... this aberration I'm going through."

"Uh-huh. Kind of like working in an ice-cream parlor when you're on a diet. Sure, go ahead. Volunteering with kids is a worthy idea. But it won't stop you longing for youngsters of your own. Little red-headed kids with blue eyes.''

Or little kids with gray eyes and baseball caps... Beck stood up. Lately she'd been finding it difficult to settle down in any one place for very long; an unaccountable restlessness had taken her over.

"Taylor, don't you have to go supervise batting practice or something?''

"Finding you a man is much more intriguing.''

"I don't want a man! I don't want baby longings! I don't want any of it!''

"You feel all right, Beck? You look flushed.''

"I'm kind of going crazy, and this dating service won't help. I suppose it's revenge for the way I've started women chasing after you.''

Taylor unwound himself from his chair. "You have the wrong idea about romance, that's your real problem. You think it's something that should come looking for you, not the other way around. You think a woman should be passive when it comes to love.''

"No way. I can't stand passive women.''

"So go for it, Beck. Go after romance. What are you waiting for?'' He strolled out of her office again, cheerful as anything. But what made Taylor McCoy such an authority on love? He was a confirmed bachelor, for goodness' sake!

Beck picked up the Find-a-Mate registration form and gazed at it contemptuously. According to the instructions, she was supposed to build her idea of the perfect man right here on paper. "Ideal height, ideal weight, preferred color of hair...''

This was ridiculous. What did hair color really matter, anyway? Today she'd hardly been able to tell the color of Taylor McCoy's hair underneath his baseball cap—

Beck dropped the form as if it were on fire. She grabbed her camera, instead, and hurried out the door. Her clown was waiting, she couldn't be late— but then she stopped and hurried back into her office again. She couldn't explain what she was doing; certainly it didn't make any sense at all. Nonetheless, she scrabbled through the pile of letters on her desk and found the bright yellow one—the one that guaranteed a five-course route to Taylor McCoy's heart via his stomach. She stuffed the letter into her bag, cursing her own irrational behavior, and sped from her office.

"FORGET THE DAMN uniform! The old one was fine. Better than fine!"

Taylor McCoy stood in the middle of the fitting room, scowling at Beck. He was wearing the Roadrunners' resplendent new uniform: burgundy piping on a soft sea-blue background. He looked awfully good in it, and Beck realized she'd chosen the colors especially with him in mind. The material of the uniform highlighted the gray of his eyes—stormy gray at the moment. Beck patiently tried to explain for the hundredth time.

"The old uniforms simply aren't attractive enough. They're too bland. They don't *say* anything. The Roadrunners need a new spruced-up image."

"The Roadrunners play baseball. They play damn well. They don't need an image!"

Beck knew Taylor wasn't just riled about the uniforms. Last night the Roadrunners had lost an important game, and it was understandable for him to be out of sorts. She wasn't taking it personally.

She raised her camera and clicked the shutter before Taylor had so much as a chance to protest. "There's nothing wrong with looking fashionable while you play ball. You should be grateful to me, Taylor. This idea of mine will take some of the attention off you for once. I'm thinking of having the team model these new uniforms for a calendar. Although of course we'll highlight the eligible bachelors. You're slated for Mr. January."

For a second there Beck feared she'd gone too far. Taylor looked like he was going to rip the burgundy trim right off his pants. Fortunately Sam Ryan of Ryan's Clothing Manufactory chose this moment to come into the fitting room. Sam was a large burly man who seemed completely at home with a tape measure draped around his neck. "Turned out good, didn't it?" he asked, surveying his creation as modeled so grudgingly by Taylor. "Needs a little work, though." Sam crouched with surprising agility and stuck some pins into Taylor's pant leg.

"Dammit, that's sewn already," Taylor protested. "Can't you leave well enough alone?"

"I'm a perfectionist," Sam said imperturbably. "Used to drive my girlfriend nuts. Ex-girlfriend, that is."

Taylor looked interested for the first time. "So you're not married, Ryan. Neither is Beck here. Quite a coincidence."

Taylor was at it again. Beck frowned at him. It was bad enough he'd started all that tomfoolery with Find-a-Mate. When Beck had categorically refused to fill out that registration form, he'd filled it out for her himself and handed it in to the dating service. She'd already received several phone calls from Find-a-Mate, claiming that the ideal man had been located for her. Beck would have nothing to do with it.

"No, Beck's not married," Taylor said. "She likes kids, though. You like kids, Ryan?"

"Sam, don't listen to him," Beck interjected. "Taylor's under the mistaken impression that he needs to find me a man as soon as possible or my biological clock will detonate."

Sam took a measurement at Taylor's ankle. "McCoy, I've known Rebecca for a while now, and I have to tell you you're fighting a lost cause. She's too picky about men. The girl has standards that make Superman look inadequate."

"That so?" For once Taylor seemed amiable to being poked with pins. "What does she expect out of a guy, anyway?"

"She's a perfectionist, like me. Now, I make a suit, I want all the lines to fall straight. Won't have it any other way. And that's how it is with Rebecca. When it comes to a man, she wants all the lines to fall straight."

Beck groaned, and both men glanced over at her. Then they went right on talking about her lamentable standards of perfection as if she wasn't even in the same room. Beck tried not to listen. Neither one of them knew a thing about her! Her standards weren't so impossible. Okay, so maybe she wanted a man who was sensitive, considerate and passionate about life. Someone who kept himself in shape, who respected his body enough to take care of it. Beck's gaze wandered down the length of Taylor's legs. The thing about baseball uniforms . . . they tended to display a man's muscles rather too nicely. . . .

Where was she? Right, her so-called impossible requirements for a man. Someday she'd meet someone. Someday she'd meet someone who'd sweep her off her feet. Beck's gaze wandered back to Taylor's muscled legs. Taylor was sensitive, of course, when he wasn't making her crazy with his matchmaking. He drove his team rigorously, but he was also considerate of each player. She remembered what he'd told her only last week: he hated it whenever he had to cut a player from the team, because he himself had been cut from the majors, and he knew how shattering it could be. Yes, Taylor was sensitive, and he had a passion. He loved baseball.

Well, perhaps someday Beck would meet someone like Taylor. Not exactly like him, of course, but close enough. She'd fall in love, get married and have those kids—all in proper order!

Beck was so lost in her own thoughts that it took her a moment to register what Sam Ryan was saying.

"Come to think of it, McCoy, you're unattached. Instead of trying to find Rebecca a man, why don't *you* take her out?"

Taylor didn't say anything, but he looked as perturbed as a hitter grounding into a double play.

"Now, wait a minute, Sam," Beck said. "I want to make one thing very clear. I'm Taylor's publicist, and that's it."

Sam walked around Taylor, tape measure flying. "Doesn't seem like such a strange idea to me. The two of you ought to get together. Romance isn't such a bad thing. I miss my ex-girlfriend, if you want to know the truth."

Taylor finally came up with an answer. "Don't forget what my publicist says, Ryan. I'm a confirmed bachelor. And from the look of things, there isn't any cure for me."

He sounded just a little too smug. Beck fished through her camera bag and brought out the bright yellow sheet of stationery she'd tucked in there.

"You might be wrong about that, Taylor. Here's someone who says there's a foolproof way to cure you. Maybe she's right. Maybe you're in more danger than you think."

"Here, let me see that." Sam took the letter and started reading it. "Hmm...this woman has the right idea. Chocolate mousse for dessert."

"What are you talking about?" Taylor read over Sam's shoulder. "I could go for the sirloin steak, but why ruin a good meal with salad?"

"She says to make the salad with endive and almonds. That's not so bad."

Beck rolled her eyes. "Okay, okay. I only showed it to you as a joke. All this stuff about getting to a man's heart through his stomach. It's ridiculous!"

Sam patted his own substantial midriff. "The woman has a point, Rebecca. Don't be so hasty to dismiss it."

Beck took the letter from him and stashed it back into her camera bag. "These are modern times," she said firmly. "A woman doesn't have to cook for a man to win his affection. It should really be the other way around. The man should cook for the woman."

Taylor shook his head. "Hey, I don't cook for anybody. Give me a deli or take-out Chinese. That's how I serve up dinner."

"Neither one of you has any imagination." Sam tugged on his measuring tape and began to look nostalgic. "I used to cook for my girlfriend. Beef curry, that was my specialty. Did the trick every time."

"I'll stick to baseball," Taylor said.

"No problem, McCoy. You don't have to do any cooking. The deal here is for *Rebecca* to supply you with a five-course meal. Why not take her up on it? What's the worst that can happen?"

"Sure, the food sounds good. But Rebecca's trouble. She's been trouble from the very beginning."

"She's cute, though. Take a look at her and tell me she's not cute."

Both men turned to gaze critically at Beck.

"Okay, so she's cute," Taylor conceded after a moment, rather gruffly. "She's darn cute. What does that have to do with anything?"

"Come on, man. See reason. How often does a pretty girl offer to cook you dinner?"

Beck could contain herself no longer. "Fellas, you seem to have overlooked one small but significant detail. I never invited Taylor to dinner!"

They both ignored her.

"Here's the deal, McCoy," said Sam. "You should treat this as a sort of scientific experiment. Think of it—some lady out there claims she's found the cure for bachelorhood. As a confirmed bachelor yourself, you're practically duty-bound to prove the woman wrong. You have to go over to Rebecca's, eat that five-course meal and show the world you can still walk away unattached."

Taylor nodded slowly, with utmost seriousness. "I'm beginning to see. I'd be doing a noble deed when it comes right down to it. I'd be acting on behalf of an entire brotherhood of confirmed bachelors, proving how strong I can be—even when tempted by a pretty girl cooking dinner."

"Now you're talking, McCoy. Bachelors everywhere will thank you for setting a good example." Sam stuck a pin into Taylor's sleeve. "It's all arranged, then. Dinner at Beck's."

"I'm glad the two of you want to save the world for bachelorhood," Beck remarked. "Sorry to disappoint you, though. Count me out of the grand experiment."

"Hey," Taylor said, "I just got into the spirit of this, and now you're going to deprive me of food...."

"Looks like it'll be another solitary night at the deli for you. Sam, if you're just about through fitting Taylor's uniform, I think we're done for the day."

"Chicken," Sam pronounced.

"I'm not cooking chicken for Taylor McCoy!"

"What I mean is—you're chicken. You're afraid even to serve the guy a home-cooked meal. Must mean you're feeling something for him you don't want to admit." Sam stuck another pin in Taylor's sleeve as if to emphasize his point.

Beck stared at both men in consternation. "That's absurd. There's nothing hidden here. I know exactly how I feel about Taylor."

Now they looked at her with sincere interest, and Beck wondered if she'd painted herself into a corner.

"Um, the truth is, I think Taylor's an excellent ... baseball manager. But I really believe him when he says he's a confirmed bachelor. Unlike every other woman in New Mexico, I don't want to convert him to the idea of marriage."

"So there's no problem." Sam smiled beneficently. "You invite McCoy to dinner, you prove you don't want him, he proves he doesn't want you—nothing could be simpler."

There was something a bit skewed about Sam's logic, but at the same time it seemed oddly persuasive. Beck didn't stop to analyze why. She brushed some lint off her camera lens. "If I did try out this so-called formula on Taylor, well, it really would prove how silly the whole thing is. Sure, we could have a good laugh over it. And maybe I can even use it as an angle for more publicity. Why not?"

"Then it's a date!" Sam proclaimed. In his own perverse underhanded way, *he* was playing match-maker, of all things.

"Want to come to dinner, too, Sam?" Beck asked. "Taylor and I are already experts on dating as a threesome."

Taylor remained impassive except for a mildly raised eyebrow, but Sam shook his head.

"Forget it. I'm going to call my ex-girlfriend right now and tell her I'm putting the curry on the stove. You two can fend for yourselves." He left the fitting room while Taylor still had pins stuck in him.

Beck suddenly realized she didn't like being alone with Taylor. She busied herself with camera paraphernalia: lens paper, cleaning fluid, canisters of film. The problem was she knew exactly why she'd allowed Sam to coerce her into this silly dinner. It *was* very simple. Underneath her protests, she really wouldn't mind spending an evening with Taylor McCoy. In fact, she looked forward to it. And she wondered if underneath his joking manner and his own protests, perhaps *he* wouldn't mind spending an evening with her, too.

At last she glanced over at him to find that he was regarding her with a rather puzzled expression. Maybe he was already sorry he'd let Sam finagle the two of them into this.

"My apartment, Saturday night, eight o'clock," she said grumpily. "But it's not too late to back out."

"I'm not backing out. Eight o'clock sounds fine. But listen, Beck—don't be worried about anything."

"What would I be worried about? If you think this is actually my attempt to cure you, you're very much mistaken. I mean, this dinner is Sam's idea, not—"

Taylor held up his hands. "Slow down. Like I said, you don't have anything to worry about. I don't suspect you of hidden motives." He grinned. "That's why I like being around you, Beck. You're the one woman I can trust right now *not* to try curing me of bachelorhood."

"Well, then." Beck popped on her lens cap and swung her camera strap over her shoulder. "I suppose Saturday night at eight will be fine. Just fine all around."

What on earth was she getting herself into?

CHAPTER SEVEN

IT WAS SATURDAY NIGHT, seven thirty-five, and Beck was in a tizzy. There was no other word for it. She'd never been in a tizzy in her life, but she certainly recognized this as one. She sped around her apartment, fluffing up the pillows on the couch, swiping at bookshelves with a dust cloth, straightening pictures on the wall, double-checking the hors d'oeuvres. At last she got control of herself, tossed the cloth under the sink where it belonged and sank into a chair. Those pictures on the walls had been crooked for months; why the need to straighten them now? Taylor wasn't going to notice.

Beck leaned back and took several deep breaths. Up until tonight, all her dealings with Taylor had been strictly on a business level. Even that one little kiss had taken place within the confines of her office....

Beck struggled out of her chair and went to examine the dining-room table. Maybe the candles were a mistake—too overtly romantic. The centerpiece was harmless enough: an Indian pottery bowl filled with violets and sprigs of greenery. Unless maybe violets could be considered romantic, too....

"Rebecca, get a grip!" she commanded herself. She hurried to her bedroom and slipped into the dress she'd laid out: a simple chemise with a belted waist.

But when she looked into the mirror, she realized the dress was all wrong. Too simple, too plain.

Berating herself, she changed into a skirt and silk shirt, ran a comb through her hair, dabbed on some perfume and hurried out to mix the salad dressing. By the time her doorbell rang at seven fifty-four, she was anything but calm. She was downright flustered and ready to call off the entire evening. But Taylor McCoy was here, waiting on the other side of the door, and there was nothing for it except to go let him in.

Taylor looked every bit the part of the proper dinner guest. He wore a narrow black tie and a nubby blue-gray jacket in a Western cut. He also proffered Beck a bottle of very good French wine.

"Hello, Rebecca," he said formally.

"Hello, Taylor," she replied, her tone equally formal. They stood facing each other in the doorway for a few seconds, neither one of them seeming to know what to say next. They'd never been at a loss for words around each other before.

"Well...please come in," Beck managed at last. "I can't have you standing out on the doorstep forever."

He came inside, glancing around rather uneasily. "Uh, nice place you have here."

"Thank you." She wasn't used to this stiff politeness with Taylor; she'd almost rather be arguing with him. But she *did* have a nice apartment, complete with brick floors and a rounded kiva fireplace presiding graciously in a corner of the living room. She felt this place represented her busy full life. Bookshelves were tucked strategically against every wall, low-maintenance cactus plants adorned a surface here and there, and attractive blinds hung at the windows, instead of fussy curtains. Every space was utilized for maximum efficiency.

Beck gestured toward the sofa. "Have a seat, Taylor. Make yourself comfortable."

The look on Taylor's face clearly expressed that comfort was a remote possibility for him at the moment. Beck almost expected him to retreat out the door before he'd so much as eaten a bite of her five-course meal. But he finally did sit down, afterward drumming his fingers on the arm of the sofa. Beck perched on the edge of a chair across from Taylor.

"Dinner'll be ready in just a little while," she said.

"Fine . . . fine." Taylor continued drumming his fingers on the sofa arm but made another valiant effort at predinner conversation. "So, Rebecca. Nice place you have here."

"I think you already mentioned that," she said helpfully.

He looked out of sorts. "Okay. So, read any good books lately?"

"Taylor, maybe we could just relax. I mean, this is only an experiment, after all. We're setting out to prove there's no such thing as a formula for romance."

He shook his head. "This is a dangerous business any way you look at it. I'm not relaxed, Beck. No way am I relaxed. Are you relaxed?"

"Not really. I've got this awful crick between my shoulders. Always happens to me when I'm tense."

"Hey, I can do something about that." Obviously relieved at the thought of action, Taylor stood and moved to behind her chair. Before she could protest, he began massaging her shoulders in matter-of-fact fashion.

His hands were strong and warm and competent. She found herself easing into his touch. "Actually, it's beginning to feel better," she admitted after a bit. She leaned her head back and gazed up at him. From this angle, she had an odd yet enticing view of his face.

Taylor gazed down at her, then abruptly halted his therapeutic massage and moved away. "Maybe we should try some other activity," he said.

She had to agree; her shoulders were tensing up all over again. Taylor glanced around with a purposeful air. Spying a magazine on the coffee table, he picked it up and read, "*Parents' Guide*. 'Your Baby's First Years,' 'Choosing a Pediatrician,' 'Building the Perfect Sandbox.' You're making this too easy for me, Rebecca. Tell me, where do you plan to put the nursery?"

She grabbed the magazine from him and slapped it back on top of her other parenting magazines, wishing she'd thought to hide the lot of them under her bed.

"In case you hadn't noticed, this place is too small for kids. When I buy my house, it'll be different—not that I'm buying a house just so I can have room for kids!"

Taylor seemed interested. "What house?"

She sighed, knowing she was just getting herself in deeper and deeper. But she led him to the room that served as her office at home, and she gestured at several of the photographs tacked up on her corkboard. The photographs depicted different views of one house—a rambling white stucco, Spanish-style, with a red tile roof. In some views, the house was half-hidden behind a wooden fence; in others, it was possible to see the vines growing up one of the walls, the big shade trees in the backyard, the rosebushes in the garden.

"Good techniques with lighting," Taylor commented. "And you really brought out some texture in this one over here."

"I don't want you to admire my photography. That's my house. Well, it's not my house yet, but it will be soon. I found it on one of my walks—For Sale sign and all. It won't be too long before I can afford to buy it. When I took the job with the Roadrunners, Alma Latham promised me a bonus if I could bring attendance at the games up to a certain level. Seems like I'm going to get that bonus, Taylor—thanks to your being such a confirmed bachelor and making the team so popular. Anyway, once I get the bonus, I'll be able to buy my house. I'm outgrowing the apartment. I simply need more room, that's reasonable enough."

Taylor clasped his hands behind his back and studied one of the photographs. "Looks like you'll have plenty of extra space."

"Three bedrooms, plus a den."

"Good-size yard, too."

Beck couldn't help getting enthusiastic. "See this tree here? It's really sturdy. The kind that's just right for climbing. I figure it's even strong enough for a tire swing. And I thought I'd put a badminton net over in that corner by the fence." She stopped when she saw the look of amusement on his face. "Listen, you don't need kids to have a swing or play badminton," she said. "The tire swing would just be a . . . a homey touch. All houses should have a tire swing as far as I'm concerned!"

He patted her on the back as if in commiseration. "It's tough, Beck. You really do have things out of order. You have the family house picked out before the family. The swing before the children. The badminton net before the—"

"Let's not go through all that again," Beck interrupted. She certainly didn't need Taylor McCoy to keep pointing out her inconsistencies. She only knew this particular house was meant for her; there wasn't a thing she could do about it. All she could do was hope she'd be able to get the down payment together before somebody else decided to buy it.

"Have you talked to Find-a-Mate yet?" Taylor asked.

"Of course not. I already told you, I'm not going to have a thing to do with your ridiculous dating service."

"Too bad. If you'd ever give Find-a-Mate a chance, you'd get yourself a man and some young'un in no time, plenty to fill your new house."

"I don't need any help from Find-a-Mate. I'll get my own man—someday."

"Planning's the key, Rebecca, whether you like it or not. You have to think ahead about these things. You can't just drift, and then wake up someday to realize you never went after your dream."

"Find-a-Mate is *not* the answer to my dreams." Beck hauled Taylor out of the room. "Come on. Let's eat dinner and be done with it."

"No need to rush things. Something tells me we're going to have a good time tonight, after all."

"I thought you said this whole idea was too dangerous."

"Yeah, but come to think of it, what's life without a little danger? I'm beginning to enjoy myself."

Beck couldn't say the same thing for herself. She wished she hadn't shown him her dream house; that hadn't been the best way to start off, sharing something private like that. Now Taylor knew more than ever how turned around her life had become.

Without ceremony, she took him to the kitchen and put the plate of hors d'oeuvres in front of him. "This is officially course number one," she announced. "Better be careful—we're talking oysters and mushrooms here. An aphrodisiac guaranteed to lower your resistance."

Taylor sampled an hors d'oeuvre with no apparent ill effect. Beck nudged the plate a little closer to him.

"Try another one," she suggested.

He eyed her speculatively. "You really want these things to work on me, Rebecca?"

"No, of course not! It's just that— Oh, for Pete's sake. Why did I ever let Sam Ryan talk me into this?"

Taylor ate another cracker with oysters and mushrooms. "Neither one of us is doing this tonight because of Sam Ryan. I know it. You know it. Why not just admit it?"

Beck pulled the plate of hors d'oeuvres back toward her. "Okay, Taylor. You tell me. Exactly why *are* we here this evening?"

"I'm here because you're...attractive. Sam did have a point when it came to that. And you're trying to find out if I might be husband material, after all."

She frowned at him. "You actually think I'm crazy enough to take any of this seriously? Maybe half the women in this state are after you, but don't flatter yourself that I'm susceptible."

"I'm not taking it personally. I figure it's something you have to get out of your system." Now Taylor was the one who frowned, looking thoughtful as he reached over to take another cracker with oysters. "Maybe the problem is, I need to get *you* out of my system, Rebecca. Maybe that's the real reason I came here tonight."

Rather uneasily Beck gave her bottle of salad dressing a good shake. "I didn't realize I *was* in your system—whatever that means." Somehow she found her gaze drawn to Taylor's mouth, and somehow she remembered exactly what it had been like to kiss him that day.

He gazed back at her, his expression grave. "I'm not sure I know what to do about you, Rebecca. I keep telling myself that you affect me a certain way because, dammit, because—I haven't been with a woman in a while. A long while," he added gruffly, rubbing his shoulder. "Not since my injury, anyway. Unfortunately that kind of... abstinence, well, it impedes a person's judgment. I thought you should know. Fair warning, that type of thing."

Beck leaned forward. "Um, how long *has* it been since your injury, Taylor?"

"About a year and a half." He reached for another hors d'oeuvre, but she snatched the plate away from him.

"Forget the oysters. It's time for the damn soup!"

Beck had made a very tasty bisque, if she did say so herself: a creamy mixture of leek, carrot and butternut squash. She sat across from Taylor at the dining-room table and watched him scrape the bottom of his bowl.

"You know, Taylor, you're even more of a confirmed bachelor than I realized. It sounds as if you've decided to stay away from women altogether. I think that shows impressive fortitude."

Taylor looked out of sorts, but didn't say a word. Beck, however, found the subject of Taylor's love life—or lack thereof—fascinating. She brought on the sirloin and potatoes.

"I'll offer some free advice," she said after serving Taylor. "Don't go telling the women of New Mexico that lately you've deprived yourself of female companionship. It'll only make them more determined than ever. You see, it makes you that much more of a challenge."

"There was nothing deprived about my sex life before my shoulder turned on me," he muttered. "Before I left the majors . . . but things are different now. Everything's different."

"Maybe they're different in a better way," Beck suggested. "And maybe you're just waiting for the right woman to happen along—not that I have any idea who the right woman is," she amended hastily, catching Taylor's suspicious glance. "It's just a possibility you can't overlook, that's what I'm trying to say. The chance that the right woman is out there for you . . . somewhere."

Taylor appeared ready to overlook the possibility entirely. He ate his steak and potatoes, refusing any further comment. Beck sat back; already a glass of Taylor's wine was making her feel a little mellow. If Taylor didn't have any women in his life at the moment, it wasn't for lack of eager candidates. The decision had to be entirely his. And knowing that only made him more appealing.

"You're a good cook, Rebecca," he said at last, almost grudgingly. "A person could get used to this."

"Don't tell me you're weakening already."

The wine seemed to have mellowed his mood, too. "I wouldn't give up bachelorhood for this—but I might be tempted."

"I'll put your mind at ease, then. I don't cook very often. I'm too busy with my work."

"Yeah, but when those kids of yours come along, you'll want to give 'em home-cooked meals. I know you, Rebecca. You want the idealized version of family life. The kind you see on the fronts of greeting cards and in television commercials."

She stabbed one of her potatoes with her fork. "My kids—when and if they come along—will be able to handle canned soup just fine."

"It won't be just can openers for you, trust me. You'll find yourself making chocolate-chip cookies, and you'll let the kids sneak cookie dough when they come home from school. I can see it, Beck, plain as anything."

She set down her fork. She knew Taylor was only teasing her, but he'd conjured up a beguiling image. Her white stucco dream house possessed a roomy kitchen with plenty of windows to let the sun stream in. She could picture herself there so easily, whipping up a batch of cookies for a passel of hungry kids. And for just a second, she pictured Taylor right along be-side her in the kitchen of her dream house, sneaking some of the cookie dough himself.

Maybe Taylor wasn't in danger of succumbing to this cure for bachelorhood, but *she* was obviously in danger. It might be best to move this meal along be-fore she had any more untoward visions about Tay-lor.

She managed to get him through the salad at a de-cent pace; he didn't like salads, so that was easy enough. But he requested two servings of dessert—it was chocolate mousse, after all—and she couldn't very well turn him down.

"Good stuff," he said. He lingered over the last serving, as if debating whether or not to ask for a third helping. She gave in and dished him up some more.

"It's my mother's recipe. I called her long-distance yesterday to find out how to make this dessert. She and my dad still live in Wisconsin—that's where I grew up."

"I bet you had lots of brothers and sisters. Maybe that's why you like kids so much."

"Just one brother, three years younger than me. No sisters. Funny, my family's not really big on kids. My parents seemed to enjoy raising us, but now they have other interests. They have their own pursuits to keep them busy, and of course that's good. They never push my brother and his wife to produce grandchildren for them. And they never seem bothered that I'm not married. I've always been glad they respected my in-dependence—until now...."

Taylor cleaned his bowl judiciously. "I see. What you want is a push from anxious parents."

"Taylor let's talk about *you* again. I see you as a kid in Little League, chasing outfield flies and making base hits like anything. I'll bet baseball was your whole life even back then."

He shrugged. "My entire family was nuts about baseball. My dad, my mom, my three brothers. Talk about team spirit—we had it. We lived in Boston, and we hardly ever missed a Red Sox game. My mother's idea of dining out was sitting us all down in a row at Fenway Park and having us eat hot dogs and cotton candy and orange slush. There's nothing like a mother who believes in junk food and baseball."

"Your parents probably didn't have any trouble encouraging you to go for a baseball career."

Taylor smiled. "That's an understatement. My brothers and I, we all played in Little League, but I was the only one serious enough about the game to keep on with it through high school and college. My parents were behind me the entire time—hardly ever missed a game. At least one or the other of them always tried to be there."

"That's exactly the way parents ought to be. You were lucky."

"Yeah, I think I was." His expression grew abstracted. "But sometimes it felt like I was playing as much for my dad as for me. I guess you could say I was living his dream. He'd always had fantasies about playing in the majors, and I was the one who made the dream come true for him. When I got cut from the team, he didn't know how to handle it at first. It was like his dream had ended, too...." Taylor stirred in his chair. "Anyway, doesn't much matter. My old man's a great guy. He thinks it's fine I'm a manager now. He can't help it if he still brags about his son who used to be a ball player.''

"You didn't let your family down, Taylor," Beck said in a soft voice. "You didn't let anybody down. You got a shoulder injury, and nobody's to blame for that."

"When you play ball, you're always on the edge. Most players strike out more times than they hit—it's just the way it is for all of us. The pressure's enormous, and in my case it didn't just come from my folks. It came from me, my teammates, the coaches—everybody. So why do I miss it so much? Why do I miss all that pressure?"

She took a moment to answer him. His love of baseball was a whole lot more complicated than she'd realized at first. She'd sensed his joy in the game, but also mixed in there somewhere were his family's aspirations for him. "Taylor, maybe the whole point is that you can have other dreams now. Maybe dreams you never thought about when you were a kid. Why not?"

He gazed at her. "I don't know, Beck. I'm still trying to figure all this out, and it's damn well not easy. But I do know that when you *have* a dream, any dream, you need to play it out. Maybe I joke around with you about this baby-hunger thing, but the truth is you ought to do something about it. You can wait all your life and keep coming up with excuses, and then it's too late. At least I'll know in the end that I went after baseball, that I gave my dream everything I had in me. Are you going to be able to say that?"

"It's not the same at all."

"Sure it is. Anytime you want something so bad it hurts, you have to go after it. You have to at least try."

Now his gaze was intense. She stared back at him, wondering if he wasn't right. Maybe she *was* being too idealistic, expecting romance to drop down in front of her. Maybe she had to go after it herself. And maybe, just maybe, the possibility of romance was closer than she'd imagined. It might be right across the table from her, needing just a little encouragement. . . .

She pushed back her chair and stood up before she could do something foolish. She knew very well that Taylor didn't want her to try finding romance with *him*. She'd really had too much wine to drink if she was even considering the possibility.

"Dinner's over," she said rather grouchily. "All five courses, and we're both still intact. So much for secret formulas." Breathing an inner sigh of relief, she led Taylor away from the table.

"Didn't that magic formula of yours say something about an old movie?" he asked. "I like old movies."

"So do I, but let's not carry this too far, okay? We tried the dinner, we proved it didn't work, and now we can go on with business as usual. I'm sure we'd both agree that's the best thing to do."

Taylor wasn't paying much attention to her. He paused in front of her television and picked up the videotape lying on top of it. *"It Happened One Night,"* he read from the label of the tape. "I'd hate to see you waste a trip to the video store."

She grabbed the tape from him and pushed it into her VCR. "Maybe we can just watch the thing on fast forward," she muttered. "After all, tomorrow's a busy day, and—"

"Tomorrow's Sunday. You don't have to work. Besides, we want to be scientific about this experiment. We need to account for all the variables." He drew her down beside him on the sofa. He'd appropriated the remote control, and soon he had Claudette Colbert and Clark Gable sparking at each other on the television screen. It *was* a good movie; how could she resist?

The pillows on the couch were comfortable. Perhaps too comfortable. Gradually, without Beck knowing quite when it happened, she found herself sitting with Taylor's arm draped over her shoulders. The atmosphere was still casual, of course. Taylor seemed intent on the movie, chuckling at the warm humorous parts. Beck laughed too, relaxing a little, settling back into the circle of Taylor's arm. This was really quite companionable, nothing to be concerned about. In fact, it was actually cozy, sharing a movie with Taylor like this.

She turned her head and smiled at him, for once harboring nothing but goodwill toward Taylor. Maybe it was the wine making her feel this benevolent, but at the moment she didn't mind.

Taylor gazed back at her, the movie apparently holding no further interest for him. He reached over to smooth a wavy strand of hair away from her forehead, and right then she knew he intended to kiss her. She also knew she didn't intend to stop him. After all, she was still feeling benevolent.

Half the enjoyment of a kiss was the anticipation. Taylor didn't appear to be in any hurry; he was obviously having a fine time savoring the preliminaries. Beck was savoring them, too. She no longer felt any need to rush through this evening. Her eyelids drifted half-shut as Taylor's fingers brushed over her cheek and then tantalized the nape of her neck. One advantage to having short hair: her nape was deliciously accessible to Taylor's touch. He leaned toward her. Beck tilted her head, and now Taylor's mouth was just a whisper from her own. But there was still no need to rush. Beck held herself in suspense, and it was at least another moment before she allowed her hands to move up over his shoulders. Perhaps now. She was yearning too much for the taste of him to delay any longer.

He kissed her, and in the background Claudette Colbert and Clark Gable sparred together unheeded. Taylor gathered Beck closer. The warmth of his lips, the silky feel of his hair under her fingers—surely these were sensations meant only for her to know. And surely he felt the same hidden longings she did....

"Taylor," she murmured. "Taylor, would it really be so terrible? You and me...domestic bliss, and all... Would it really be so bad?"

CHAPTER EIGHT

BECK'S QUESTION seemed to hover in the air, but Taylor left no doubt that the kiss was over. He straightened away from her, his face taking on a look of extreme discomfiture. "Dammit, Rebecca, not you, too. I thought you were the one woman I could trust!"

She squirmed over to a more neutral position on the couch. "I was only posing a hypothetical question," she grumbled. "It's nothing for you to get all worked up about."

"What am I supposed to answer?" Taylor stood up, no doubt expecting her to sneak a wedding ring onto his finger at any moment. "Am I supposed to say I want a wife and kids—just like that, problem solved?"

"Look, I don't want you to solve any of *my* problems. I don't need the favor. Besides, it was the oysters talking, the wine...I don't know. But the way I recall it, you're the one who started all the romantic stuff tonight. It wasn't me!"

Taylor didn't seem to be listening. He paced back and forth in front of the TV, the black-and-white figures on the screen flickering behind him.

"A baseball career is bad enough. All your life, you dream so much about playing that it tears you up inside. All you can think about is getting to the majors, making it to the show. Then, if you're lucky enough, if you really do make it, the dream's over too soon. But you can't stop dreaming, and it still tears you up inside. I'm supposed to bring a wife and kids into all that?''

''Taylor.'' Beck went to him and touched his arm. ''You're not supposed to do anything. You're just supposed to sit down with me and watch the rest of the movie. And we'll have a good laugh about what I said, and then we'll forget all about it.''

He stared at her, a bleakness in his expression that made her heart ache.

''I can't give you what you want, Rebecca. Hell, I wish I could. I wish I could make that ideal vision of family life come true for you. But it's not going to happen.''

''I keep telling you. I don't *want* to feel this way. I don't want to need so much...''

''But you do need it. Just don't waste your time looking for it with the wrong guy.''

''Taylor...''

This time he drew away when she touched him. ''I have to go, Beck. Thanks for the dinner. It was great. The whole damn evening was great. I just have to get out of here.''

After he left, Beck sat for a long while on the sofa, staring at the movie on her television screen. She watched as Claudette and Clark finally found their happy ending, the walls between them tumbling down at last. Beck didn't think that was ever likely to happen with her and Taylor. He was hurting inside, but he wouldn't let anyone help him—least of all her. Darn it! What had possessed her to open her mouth and blurt out that nonsense about domestic bliss? It had only complicated everything. She was beginning to act as if she had no sense at all. Why, she was beginning to act like all those other women who wanted to win Taylor McCoy. Anyone would think Beck was falling for her own publicity campaign!

She'd had her fill of magic formulas—five-course dinners guaranteed to pave the road to a man's heart. She would never try such a thing again, not even in jest. Magic formulas could jumble your life around, make it even more topsy-turvy than it had been before. No, from now on Beck was going to stick to real solutions.

She went to clear away the dishes from the table. She went to clear away every remnant of the meal she'd shared with Taylor McCoy.

BECK DROVE SLOWLY down a country lane in Albuquerque's north valley, scanning the addresses on mailboxes. It was a beautiful, peaceful area of town: honeysuckle spilling over the tops of walls, slender morning-glory vines tangling on the ground or climbing up fences, bright red clusters of chili peppers—*ristras*—hanging in the doorways of houses. She could well understand why Taylor had chosen to live in this neighborhood.

It had been three weeks since the night he'd eaten dinner at her house—three tense and uncomfortable weeks. Things between the two of them had definitely changed, and not for the better. Whenever they met at the ballpark, the atmosphere between them was strained. They were polite to each other, certainly, but that was what bothered Beck the most. She was coming to detest politeness and all the rigid barriers it could erect between two people. It was about time Taylor heard an *im*polite thing or two from her! It was about time he heard a lot of things. After all, Beck had just made the most important, and perhaps the most terrifying, decision of her life. In a strange way Taylor had helped her to come to that decision, and it was something she wanted to tell him about.

At last she spotted his address, and she turned into a gravel drive to park next to his old green truck. His house was a two-story adobe, with an inviting flagstone patio in front. Beck crossed the patio and raised the knocker against the carved wooden door, but no answer came. She went around to the back, where the yard spread out into a spacious field. Taylor was in a corral, running a brush down the glossy flank of a roan horse.

The horse noted Beck's presence first, raising his graceful head and shaking his mane. Taylor looked up a second later, and immediately his expression became wary. Goodness, these days he behaved as if any moment he expected to see Beck arranged in full bridal regalia, coming to drag him down the aisle.

"Don't worry," she called to him. "I'm unarmed. No wedding veil. No bouquet. You're safe for the present."

It was impossible to tell if Taylor was reassured. He merely watched her approach, a vaguely dissatisfied expression on his face. The horse greeted her with a lot more enthusiasm than Taylor, nuzzling her shoulder when she came near.

"Easy there, Davy," Taylor murmured. "Give the lady some space. You should always give a lady plenty of room."

"Unlike you, he knows I'm harmless." Beck put her hand out to the horse. "Wish I had a carrot for him."

"I know what he'd like." Taylor went to one of the fruit trees along the fence, plucked an apple and brought it to Beck. "Here, you give it to him."

She clutched the apple and offered it rather uncertainly. "I've never done this before..." The horse's mouth looked awfully big. Beck didn't even want to think about the size of his teeth.

"There's a technique," Taylor said. "Hold the apple out flat in your hand... That's good. Now bring it around under his mouth or he won't be able to reach it... There you go."

It turned out to be surprisingly pleasant, having a horse snuffle an apple from her hand. After he'd chomped it, Beck ran her fingers over his forelock. The horse nudged her shoulder once more, seemingly uninterested in his master now.

"Traitor," Taylor said, working his brush over Davy's back. "So, Rebecca. What brings you out this way?"

"Darn it, you're doing it again."

"Doing what?"

"You've being civil. I'd rather hear you yell, just so we could have a real conversation for once. That's why I came, Taylor. So we could have a real conversation."

"Fire away. I'm listening."

Now that the moment had arrived, Beck hesitated. She could feel her heart pounding, and she glanced around rather desperately.

"Uh, Taylor, this is a pretty good spread you have here. I like it."

"I just took the place on a six-month lease. It has room for Davy, but maybe next year I'll have to board him at a stable again. You never know what's going to happen in baseball. Here today, gone tomorrow. But now you're the one hiding behind small talk. What gives?" Taylor gazed at her intently, although he went on grooming his horse. Beck was glad of that; there was something soothing about the long gentle strokes of the brush over Davy's coat.

"Okay, here goes. First off, you should know I called Find-a-Mate a couple of weeks ago. I agreed to let them set me up on a date."

Taylor's brush paused on Davy's back. "Finally doing something about your man problem. How'd it go?"

It annoyed Beck that Taylor continually referred to her as having a man problem. "If you want to know the truth, it was awful. Find-a-Mate's idea of my ideal partner was an architect who spent the entire evening telling me how talented and brilliant he was, and how someday his boss was going to be sorry for not showing more appreciation."

Davy nickered a bit imperiously, and Taylor went on brushing. "Sometimes an idea doesn't pan out exactly the way you'd like. Doesn't mean you should stop trying."

Beck stuffed her hands into the pockets of her skirt and gave Taylor an acid look. "I did keep trying...and trying. I figured I was going to give Find-a-Mate a real chance. So I went to a roller-skating rink with a driving instructor who already has two ex-wives and who swears he can tell by the way I drive that I have unresolved hostility toward men. And after that

I went to a concert with an ophthalmologist who was very nice, but just when I was starting to enjoy myself, he told me he was hopelessly in love with one of his neighbors. He keeps giving her the wrong prescription for contact lenses so she'll have to come back to his office. The poor woman probably has double vision by now."

Taylor chuckled, then made a concerted effort to appear sympathetic. "Hey, the important thing is that you're getting out there, starting to meet guys. You'll find the right one before you know it."

Beck didn't tell Taylor that she couldn't avoid making a mental comparison every time she met a man—and that she couldn't help noting that no man seemed as dynamic or vital as Taylor himself.

"Look, the only reason I'm telling you any of this— well, frankly I'm embarrassed about what happened that night you came for dinner at my place. But at least it made me realize I need to take matters into my own hands. That's why I tried Find-a-Mate, and it just confirmed all my suspicions that you can't force romance."

"You've got to give things more of a chance. It's like I'm always telling my players—"

"I'm not one of your players, Taylor. Hear me out on this. I've been trying something else these past few weeks. I started volunteering at an elementary school, giving classes in photography. I thought it would help me figure out a little better how I feel about children. And it did. It helped me see that no matter how much I love being around other people's kids, I want children of my own." Beck took a deep breath. "So now it's on to the next step. Taylor... I've decided to adopt a baby.''

There. She'd said it, and spoken out loud, it didn't sound so frightening anymore. It sounded quite ordinary and wonderful at the same time. She said the words again, for good measure. "I've decided to go ahead and adopt a child on my own."

It sounded even better the second time, but Taylor's expression had turned grave. He set down his brush and let Davy out of the corral. The horse trotted over to a clump of hay, unmindful of either Beck or Taylor now that more food was in the offing.

Taylor took Beck's arm and steered her toward the house. "Come on. I think I'd better get you out of the sun."

"I haven't lost my senses, you know. I've given this a great deal of thought. I know what I'm doing, Taylor."

"It's not like you to give up on romance," he muttered. "This is serious. Very serious." He ushered her through the back door and into his kitchen. The air was kept cool by the thick adobe walls, refreshing after the heat outside. Allowing no protests, Taylor prodded Beck down into a chair and began scrounging in his refrigerator. After a moment he produced a couple of soft drinks.

"Here, try one of these. Maybe you're dehydrated."

"I'm *fine*. I thought you'd be happy for me. You're the one who's always telling me to go after what I want, instead of just dreaming about it. This is what I want—a family."

He sat down across from her, propping his elbows on his knees and clasping his hands around a soda bottle. "Dammit, I know you want a family. But not this way. You want the greeting-card version. The guy who falls in love with you, the kids who come along afterward. How can you turn your back on that?"

He really did seem disturbed, as if she had personally assaulted *his* ideal of family life.

"I'm not turning my back on anything," she said quietly. "I'll always know what I want a family to be like. And maybe someday I'll find the romantic kind of love I need. But I'm not putting my life on hold until then. I want a kid, Taylor. Boy, do I want a kid! It feels good to finally say that wholeheartedly. Maybe I'm crazy, but I think I'd make a good mother."

"Okay, so Find-a-Mate didn't work out. What about a skeet-shooting class? You're bound to meet plenty of men that way."

She stared at him in exasperation. "You're the one who told me if I wanted a kid, I should just have a kid and not wait for any man. What's come over you?"

He rubbed his hands on his jeans. "Hell, it's simple. I've changed my mind. I want you to have your dream, that's all. Not a half-baked version of it, but the whole ballyhoo. People lose their dreams enough as it is. You shouldn't settle for less from the very beginning."

Beck wondered what a "ballyhoo" was; it sounded enticing. She sighed. "Taylor, I'm twenty-eight years old. I suppose I could wait until I'm thirty-eight or forty-eight or whatever. But I want to give something to a child before my hair turns gray. I want to enjoy a child *now*. And I have a feeling that somewhere out there is a baby who needs me, too. So I'm going through with this. I have an appointment at an adoption agency this afternoon. An hour from now to be exact."

Taylor didn't say anything for a long time, but then he stirred. "What about your career? How are you going to have time for that and a baby, too? Especially without any help from a husband."

"I've considered all of that, and I have it figured out. My big advantage is that I'm self-employed. I can arrange to work at home as much as possible. Of course, I'll use baby-sitters when it's necessary. I realize how much work it's going to be, but I'll handle it."

Taylor didn't appear convinced. "What about money? Without a husband's contribution, raising a kid will drain everything you've got. You'll put yourself in a damn precarious position, Beck."

"I know what I'm doing," she repeated. She stood, thumping her bottle of soda pop down on the table. "I didn't come here to defend myself to you. I came because, well, the funny thing is, without you I don't think I would've made this decision. You helped me see my life can't always be perfect, but I should just go ahead with my dreams, anyway. So, thanks." She headed for the door.

"Beck, wait." Taylor moved to block the way. "You do seem pretty set on this," he said grudgingly. "Since I can't talk you out of it, I'd like to go on that appointment with you."

She gazed at him in surprise. "Why on earth ...?"

"Don't you need a character witness, or something? I'd better come."

"I appreciate this, Taylor, but it's not necessary."

"I don't need to be at the ballpark until after six tonight. My coaches can handle the warm-up. All I need is to change my clothes and I'll be ready to go. Wait here, Beck."

She'd often seen Taylor like this—decisive, taking charge of his players, marshaling the starting lineup for a game. Now he seemed to be marshaling her for her appointment. She wanted to argue about it, but he was already striding out of the kitchen. And, truth was, she hadn't found it easy to reach her decision. In a way it was a relief to know that Taylor was offering his support—even if he didn't approve of what she was doing.

That was the real surprise, Taylor's resistance toward her decision. She'd assumed he'd clap her on the back in congratulations and be relieved to see her off to the adoption agency. After all, what better proof could he have that she truly harbored no hopes of converting him from bachelorhood?

The important thing was that no one could talk her out of her decision—not Taylor McCoy, not anyone. She knew there was a child somewhere who needed her; she just knew it. That conviction was what had made her pick up the phone and call the adoption agency. She couldn't turn back now; she didn't want to turn back.

Beck tried drinking the rest of her soda, but it had gone flat. She poured it down the sink, noting the clutter of dirty dishes piled there. She smiled a little. Taylor was a bachelor, all right, and bound to remain so. Maybe he'd never put down roots anywhere; he'd load Davy into a trailer and simply go wherever baseball happened to take him. That seemed to be what he wanted, anyway. Beck splashed water on his dishes, then told herself firmly it was no concern of hers if he left macaroni to dry on his plate all night.

He appeared a few moments later, wearing his tan jacket and a silk print tie. He looked commanding and businesslike—persuasive. Too bad *he* wasn't the one adopting.

"Taylor, this is ridiculous. If I'm going to raise a kid on my own, I have to start out by myself, too."

"You need me along. And from the sound of things, I'm pretty much responsible for putting the idea of Baby Danley into your head."

"I wouldn't go that far—"

"Come on, Beck. We don't want to be late for this appointment. We'll discuss strategy along the way."

Beck was too nervous about the appointment to fight him anymore. She followed him outside and watched as he lifted up his garage door, revealing a dark sleek sedan—an elegant car about as different from his truck as a vehicle could get.

"Don't drive it much," he said, looking the expensive sedan over with an expression almost of distrust. "But we're trying to make a good impression today. Can't take any chances."

A few seconds later Beck sank back against the velvety upholstery of the car, seeking the headrest. This luxury was just what she needed. Surely she'd do a lot better at the agency if she was relaxed for her interview. As Taylor pulled out of the drive, she glanced toward his truck. Trust him to own a sophisticated car like this, but to drive his muddy old pickup most of the time. She was beginning to know a few things about

Taylor. He preferred the low-key and unpretentious every time. His horse was a case in point. Davy wasn't a thoroughbred, or a show pony. He was just your good, basic horse, roan coat glossy from all that brushing.

Beck gave Taylor the address of the agency, then settled back again. But he wouldn't let her relax.

"I understand these adoption people can be pretty tough," he said. "The way I figure it, you gotta go in there bursting with confidence. Show them you won't take no for an answer."

She sat up straighter. "So why did you just spend all that time in your house, grilling me and trying to tear *down* my confidence? You're making me nuts today."

"Beck, I'd still talk you out of this if I could. But as long as you're going to do it, you might as well give it everything you've got."

"Right, right. As long as I'm at bat, I'd better swing damn hard."

He looked pleased. "You have the right idea, Rebecca. Definitely the right idea."

The adoption agency was located in a neat brick office complex near the foothills of the Sandia Mountains. Inside the waiting room, the windows afforded a striking panorama of the mountains, yet Beck found the other people in the room more interesting than any scenic view. They were all couples— some older, some younger, but still…all couples. Beck figured she was the only single person applying to adopt. She sat with fists clenched in her lap until Taylor reached over and smoothed out one of her hands in his own. She welcomed this silent gesture of support, taking comfort in the warmth of his touch. But then she realized the irony of it: to any casual observer, she and Taylor would appear to be a couple, too—a husband and wife, beginning the adoption procedure together. Talk about false impressions! Beck quickly slipped her hand away from Taylor's.

They had to wait quite a while, but at last Beck's name was called. She and Taylor were shown into a small cubbyhole of an office, and a moment later a harried-looking woman came in.

"Ms. Danley? I'm Nina Hughes. Sorry to keep you so long. We really are very busy around here. Always running behind— Why, you're that fellow in the newspapers—the confirmed bachelor. Saw your picture just yesterday."

Beck's publicity campaign was certainly reaching into all corners of the city, but Taylor didn't seem too happy about that. He gave Beck a resentful glance. Meanwhile, Nina Hughes settled behind her desk with a flurry of papers.

"Where *are* my notes? Always so much to do in this place... Ah, here we are. Rebecca Danley." Nina slipped on a pair of glasses and scanned a scribbled page. "Ms. Danley, we spoke briefly on the phone, but I understood you wished to adopt on your own. I didn't realize the 'confirmed bachelor' would be a participant...."

Taylor started to answer, but Beck intercepted him. "Mr. McCoy is a...a friend," she said hastily. "He's here only in that capacity. I *am* adopting on my own."

"I see." Nina slipped off her glasses and pinched the bridge of her nose. She had the look of someone who'd been jogging on a treadmill for hours and didn't see any jumping-off point in sight. "Very well, Ms. Danley. We'll proceed, but I'm sure you realize we must give preference to married couples. We have such a long waiting list, as it is."

"I do realize—" Beck started to murmur, but this time Taylor took over.

"Rebecca understands the difficulties faced by any single parent, but you'll find that she's an excellent prospect for your agency. After today, you'll want to put her at the top of your list."

Nina Hughes let her gaze settle on Taylor. "Is that so. You know, Mr. McCoy, I haven't been to a ball game since I was a teenager. These days I never seem to have the time."

"Come out and see the Roadrunners, Ms. Hughes. I guarantee you won't be sorry. We're aiming for the pennant this year."

Nina sighed wistfully. "You know what I like about a baseball game? You just...sit. You just sit there and watch it. You don't have to do anything."

"So come on out and sit," Taylor said in a genial tone.

Beck cleared her throat, perhaps a bit too forcefully. "Ms. Hughes, about the adoption..."

"Yes, yes, of course." Nina slid her glasses on and sifted through her papers again. "Tell me about Danley Public Relations. Self-employment always raises a red flag to us, I'm afraid. The possibility of erratic income, irregular hours, that sort of thing."

Beck opened her mouth, but this time she didn't even get a word out before Taylor spoke.

"Ms. Hughes, Rebecca's had a long-term commitment to her business. She's well established in Albuquerque, with a number of steady clients. Her income isn't a problem, and self-employment means she can arrange her hours to be with the baby. Can't ask for better than that, can you?"

Beck stared at Taylor. To listen to him, you'd never know that only a short while ago he'd raised the very same objections as Nina Hughes. But didn't he realize Beck could speak for herself, darn it?

Nina didn't seem to mind conversing with Taylor. She slipped her glasses off once again. "Taylor, you might as well call me Nina. Let's not be so formal here. Oh, don't worry, I'm not interested in changing your bachelor status. I have a husband, and three kids to boot."

"Three kids? Any Little Leaguers?"

"They're all girls. Soccer team, two of them."

Taylor shook his head. "Soccer's fine, but there's nothing like baseball. It's a damn shame girls aren't encouraged to play."

Beck coughed. "I wouldn't mind raising a girl of my *own*," she hinted.

Nina's glasses went back on. "Let's discuss housing arrangements. I believe you told me you're currently living in an apartment and have plans to purchase a house. I'm afraid that's a little uncertain. We'd want to see you definitely settled in a home suitable for a child."

"It's a done deal, Nina," Taylor said. "Rebecca has the house all picked out, and it's just a matter of wrapping up the details."

Beck glared at him. Just a matter of wrapping up the details! She wouldn't have her bonus from the Roadrunners until the end of the baseball season. The last thing she wanted to do was mislead the adoption agency. That wouldn't help her cause any.

"Ms. Hughes," she began. "Nina, that is. What Taylor means to say—"

"It's a fine house," he said. "Room for a tree swing in the backyard, and Rebecca's going to put up a badminton net. Any kid would be glad to grow up there."

Nina hesitated, then shook her head. "Rebecca, I simply have to be honest with you. I'm not optimistic. Being single and self-employed will stand against you, no matter what. It could take years for you to get a baby."

The disappointment Beck felt was a physical sensation, a heaviness deep inside her. Perhaps until this moment she hadn't realized how much she wanted this. How much she truly wanted to raise a child and make a family of her own.

This time she was the one who reached out to Taylor, clasping his hand tightly. This time, without questioning, she took the support he silently offered.

CHAPTER NINE

TAYLOR WENT ON HOLDING Beck's hand, but he leaned forward in his chair. "I just don't buy it. Rebecca would make a damn good parent. She deserves this chance."

"I'm genuinely sorry," Nina said. "If it was only up to me, I'd have a baby here for Rebecca tomorrow. Anyone who wants a child enough to raise one on her own... Personally, I'll admit I'm swayed by that. Since I have children, I know what a tremendously difficult job it is. But I also know how much happiness it can bring."

"Then convince your supervisors," Taylor said. "Let's get that kid for Rebecca."

"I'm willing to do whatever it takes," Beck added. "I'll do anything to prove I should be a mother. Just tell me what else I need."

Nina gave a reluctant shrug. "I wish it was that simple. But it's not. Really, the only thing that could help you right now is producing a husband. My supervisors would feel a whole lot better knowing a father would be around to raise the child, too."

Taylor chose this moment to stand up. "There has to be a way around all this," he muttered. "Wait a minute. We've been thinking babies. What if Beck was willing to adopt an older child?"

Nina Hughes rubbed the bridge of her nose more energetically this time. She put her glasses on, only to pop them off again a second later. "That would change the situation. I assumed you wanted a baby, and babies are always in short supply. But an older child... Rebecca, you haven't said anything. How do you feel about it?"

Being around Taylor today seemed to render Beck speechless a good deal of the time. But at last she found her voice. "I was only considering the possibility of a baby, too. I thought I had to start everything off from the very beginning. That's the way it's usually done." She glanced at Taylor, then glanced quickly away again. "I was trying to arrange at least a few things in my life in the proper order."

"You've always said you liked nine- and ten-year-olds," Taylor pointed out. "All those kids you photograph at birthday parties, they're about that age."

"It's awfully scary," she said, even as the idea began to take hold of her, "a kid coming to me already half-grown. Would I be able to handle that?"

"It's true that older children have special problems," Nina said. "Most likely they've been hurt, one way or another, and a lot of times they feel abandoned. Winning their trust isn't easy, even though such children want a family more than anything. I can understand if you'd like to think about it."

Beck had never been this scared—and yet, oddly enough, she'd never been this certain of anything before. Somehow Taylor had brought this adoption into perfect focus. Beck stood up and this time she gazed steadily at him, without looking away.

"An older child would be perfect, just perfect."

Taylor gazed back at her with an expression she couldn't read. She'd seen pain in his eyes before, but this was different. Almost a regretfulness, perhaps.

"I think you're going to be happy, Beck," he murmured. "I think this will work out for you, after all."

Nina rustled more papers. "We'll start the preliminaries, then. It'll still be a somewhat lengthy process, Rebecca. We'll want to make sure you end up with the child that's right for you. Creating permanent families is our biggest concern."

Beck smiled ruefully. "It happens to be my biggest concern, too."

Nina reached across the desk to shake hands. "You'll be hearing from me, Rebecca. And, Taylor, one way or another, I'll get my husband and kids out to the ballpark for some serious sitting. Just win that championship for us."

It wasn't until Beck and Taylor were in the car and driving away that the enormity of it all struck home. This time Beck really needed the headrest.

"My whole life is going to change! Every single bit of it. I wonder—do all prospective parents feel this way? Like they're going to dance one minute and scream the next?"

"Dancing and screaming...I wouldn't know," Taylor said.

"You sure managed to take charge in there, but now I guess I'm grateful. You're the one who came up with the solution."

"Beck, I still wish you were doing this the regular way, the way you really want. Some things you shouldn't miss out on. Sure, adopting an older kid is a nice idea, but that kid ought to have a father, as well as a mother. I keep coming back to that."

"I'm doing the best I can—things being so out of order and all. You have any more suggestions, Taylor?"

"I'm all out of them for the day...."

THE PLUSH GRAY ELEPHANT had a wobbly trunk and floppy ears. Beck sat on her sofa, holding the latest stuffed animal she'd been unable to resist in the toy store. She gazed at the little elephant as if it could give her the wisdom she needed for raising another human being. Only last week she'd had a call from the adoption agency. Things were moving along more quickly than anticipated; it was possible that a seven-year-old girl had been found. A social worker would be coming out to talk to Beck and give her more details.

A little girl, seven years old . . . Oh, Lord, could she really be the kind of mother any kid needed? Back and forth Beck went with that question. One minute she was soaring with confidence, and the next swirling in doubts. She'd heard that being in love was a little like this. Maybe having kids was easier if you'd been in love first....

Beck impatiently tweaked an elephant ear. Of course it was better to be in love first! Of course it was better to find a husband and then have a child. But she couldn't wait around forever, hoping her life would fall into just the right pattern. Now she'd taken charge of things, and it felt good. It felt darn good—when she wasn't scared out of her socks by the responsibility ahead of her.

Beck left the little elephant tucked in a corner of the sofa and went into her office. She settled down at the desk and flipped open her notebook. A long to-do list confronted her: she had to check with the printer about the special-edition baseball programs for the Roadrunners, confirm arrangements for the country-western singer performing at the Saturday game, make sure the team had enough T-shirts and baseballs to give away at next week's charity promotion. And then there were Beck's other clients—her birthday-party clown who had a big performance coming up at the state fair, the eighteen-year-old fledgling actor who'd just landed a part with a community theater, the gardening expert who was trying to break into local TV... and Taylor McCoy.

Taylor didn't belong in her thoughts, but he kept intruding, anyway. Beck pushed aside her to-do list and swiveled to gaze out the window. A new constraint had entered her relationship with Taylor. He was always interested to hear the latest news about the adoption proceedings, but then he would become aloof, as if he regretted his own part in encouraging the adoption. He'd made his views very clear: he thought Beck should meet the right man before things went any further. And he categorically refused to be the right man himself.

Of course, he wasn't the right man. He didn't want a family in any shape or form, so he couldn't be right. He wanted baseball, not romance. So why couldn't she stop thinking about him for one solitary second?

She swiveled back to her desk, picked up the phone and called the printer. Yes, the galleys of the program were ready for her to review. She called her clown.

Yes, his new fluorescent nose was a real hit with the kids. She called the eighteen-year-old actor. No, the dress rehearsal for the play wasn't until tomorrow—

Her doorbell rang, interrupting this spate of work. Beck pushed back her chair and went to the front door. Taylor stood on her stoop, wearing a smile and holding a bandanna.

"Turn around, Beck," he commanded.

"What...?"

But already he was turning her around himself, placing the bandanna over her eyes as a blindfold. He tied a knot at the back of her head.

"Taylor, what are you doing? I don't have time to play games."

"This is no game," he said. "Come on, I'm taking you somewhere. But it's a surprise."

"That much is obvious." She clung to Taylor as he led her out to the parking lot and boosted her into his truck. A second later they were rattling down the street, and Beck tried peeling up a corner of her blindfold.

"No cheating," he warned. "I want this to be an authentic surprise."

"Believe me, Taylor, everything about you is that!" Secretly, Beck loved surprises. And she didn't have long to wait for this one. Taylor drove only a short distance before pulling over. He helped Beck from the truck and guided her along some sort of path.

"Can I look yet?"

"No, not yet.... Okay...now!" He untied the bandanna and slipped it away from her with a flourish. Beck found herself standing in front of the house.

Her house. White stucco walls, red tile roof, blue trim at the windows. And no For Sale sign.

"Taylor—"

"It's yours, Beck, all yours. Ready for the Danley family to move in anytime." He sounded very satisfied with his surprise.

She sank down on the front porch steps and drew up her knees. "All right, Taylor, why don't you tell me exactly what's going on here?"

He pushed back his baseball cap. "It's pretty self-evident—I bought the house for you. Your secretary helped me out a little—she gave me the phone number of the Realtor you'd been talking to. Anyway, we can't wait for that bonus of yours to come in, not when you've got social workers sprouting everywhere and wondering what the kid's home is going to be like. Don't worry, Beck, it's all aboveboard. Once you have the bonus, you pay me back. Couldn't be more simple."

Beck didn't know what to say. No, that wasn't true. She knew *exactly* what to say. She jumped up and confronted him.

"Taylor, you can't do this! I'm adopting a child on my own, not with you. And I can afford to do it on my own. I don't need your help."

"Calm down. I told you, this is just a temporary measure. At the end of the season, Alma pays your bonus, then you pay me. Meanwhile, we've got the place under wraps. Maybe you didn't realize it, but a retired colonel was interested in buying this house. The Realtor told me I was lucky I called when I did." Taylor still sounded awfully happy with himself. Beck propped her forehead against one of the white stucco walls and took several deep breaths.

"Okay, Taylor, I'll start again. Part of me is truly... touched that you'd go to all this trouble for me. But the other part is mad as hornets that you'd interfere at all! The whole point is that I want to do the adoption on my own. I *need* to do it on my own."

"Hell, what you need is a man, and you know it."

Beck lifted her head. "Are you volunteering for the job?" she asked sarcastically.

He folded his arms across his chest. "I'm trying to help out a little, that's all. No crime in that."

Beck stuffed her hands into the pockets of her jeans and walked along the borders of the flower beds. The irises had long since stopped blooming, the tips of their leaves turned brown with the first hint of fall. The roses, however, burned crimson and orange against the trellis. Ever since she'd first seen the house, Beck had planned to expand the flower garden and put in some vegetables, too—tomatoes and green beans. Plus, she'd always harbored a particular longing to have a pumpkin patch. This house was meant to be hers, and Taylor McCoy, confound him, had just made sure that it *was* hers. How could he be so infuriating and wonderful at the same time?

"I'd hate to see the place go to somebody else, just because baseball season isn't over yet," she admitted reluctantly. "And it's true I can pay you back in just a few weeks. I guess I'm saying thank you again, Taylor. This is one more thing that's not happening the way I'd like it, but I'm saying thank you, anyway. I mean, it was really thoughtful of you."

He seemed uncomfortable. "I didn't do it so you'd thank me. I did it because . . . I had a good time doing it, that's all." He came to her, spread open her palm and placed a key there. "Are we going inside or what, Rebecca?"

"We're going inside." She was filled with a sense of excitement—and homecoming—as she turned the key in the lock. She'd been through the house before, but always with a Realtor hovering nearby. This time was different. This time she and Taylor were taking possession of the place.

The house had been standing empty a few months, and the rooms were bare of furniture. Beck liked that because it allowed her to enjoy the airy lines of the architecture. She walked slowly around the living room as Taylor watched from the doorway.

"This carpet will have to go, of course," she said. "I'd like area rugs, instead. But I can't decide whether to paint or wallpaper in here. What do you think?"

"It's your roost, you can do whatever you want."

For a moment there Beck had experienced the odd conviction that it was *their* house, hers and Taylor's. Again she was struck by the irony of her relationship with him. If anyone were to peek through the windows right now, she and Taylor would appear to be a married couple touring their first home together. A married couple getting ready to start a family all their own. . . .

Beck moved restlessly to the next room, talking to cover the ache inside her. "I know this is supposed to be a formal dining area, but I've never liked that kind of thing. Instead, I thought this could be a play area for... for my child. That way my office will be close by, over there—"

"Hey, I almost forgot." Taylor went to a bucket of ice in the corner and held up a bottle of champagne. "I thought we'd share a toast."

She wasn't going to cry, was she, for goodness' sake? She blinked quickly, but she couldn't help thinking this was how a married couple would celebrate their house, especially if the husband happened to have a romantic turn of mind.

"Don't lose track of real life," Beck muttered to herself. Taylor glanced at her sharply but didn't say anything. He popped the cork from the bottle and poured the champagne into two glasses. He and Beck clicked the glasses together awkwardly.

"Here's to your new house," he said. "Here's to your new future."

Beck couldn't see clearly into the future, not clearly at all. Yet she seconded the toast. "Here's to your own future, wherever it happens to take you. But Alma Latham hopes you're going to stay right here, with the Roadrunners."

"I think she'd better wait to see if we win the pennant."

Beck sat down cross-legged on the floor with her champagne. "You know she wants you to stay no matter what. She likes the job you're doing."

Taylor sat down opposite her, propping himself against the wall. "I don't know what'll happen yet. There's a chance I could get a job as a scout for one of the major-league clubs. It would mean a lot of travel, but I like to travel."

"I guess you should do whatever seems best for your career." Beck spoke stiffly. She'd just assumed that Taylor would stay on as manager of the Road-runners. Not that she imagined anything could happen between the two of them, of course, but she'd liked thinking he would be in Albuquerque.

"It's not about my career," he said. "Careerwise, my job with the Roadrunners is fine, just fine."

"So what *is* it about? Why wouldn't you stay in New Mexico for another season?"

He shifted his back against the wall, as if he didn't know how to get comfortable. "The truth is…maybe even that job as scout isn't right for me. I don't know if I can be around baseball anymore, Beck. That's the thing. Managing, coaching, but not being able to play—that's all I ever wanted to do, play ball. And it's gone. If I just got away entirely, maybe I wouldn't remember anymore what it feels like…to win." His voice was low and filled with the pain she'd come to recognize.

"Taylor, I know you. Turning your back on baseball is the last thing you should do."

"Right now it seems like the best thing."

Neither one of them spoke for a while, but then Taylor broke the silence.

"You told me the agency called you. Did they give you some more details?"

"They have a little girl named Elizabeth. That sounds like such a big name for a child. Anyway, she's seven, and she's been in foster care for years. Her mother was very young and didn't want anything to do with the child."

"Kid's had a rough life already."

"You could say that. But she's been lucky to have stable foster parents. They're an older couple and can't really afford to keep the children they take in. Apparently they're more like grandparents to Elizabeth than anything else."

"So when do you get to meet her?"

Beck reached up and traced a finger through the dust on one of the window sills. "Hopefully next week. I'll be honest, Taylor—I'm scared to death. A little seven-year-old girl, and I'm quaking in my shoes."

He tapped his glass on the floor. "Look, you don't have to go through this by yourself, you know. I'd be glad to meet the kid with you. Sometimes two people can handle a situation together better than one person alone."

Beck hesitated. "I don't think that's a good idea. I don't want Elizabeth to get the impression from the very beginning that... I just don't think it's a very good idea!"

"All right, I see your point. But the kid's going to see me sooner or later. I'll be around."

"Will you, Taylor?"

"Sure. Even if I leave New Mexico, I'll be coming to Albuquerque some of the time. And I'll drop in to see you. I'll want to know how you're doing. I'm not going to lose touch, Beck."

"Just send me a Christmas card now and then. It'll be enough." She scrambled to her feet, almost knocking over her glass of champagne. Taylor rose to stand beside her, taking her hand.

"Dammit, I care what happens to you. Is that so bad?"

"You want to be my friend, Taylor? Is that it?"

"I don't know what the hell I want."

"Maybe you'd better figure it out, then. Because when I finally do adopt a child, I don't want her confused by anything. She's going to need certainty, things she can count on." Beck stalked into the kitchen and scowled at all the lovely cabinet space, then gazed out the window to the back. There it was, just as she'd always imagined in her mind: a tire swing hanging from the sturdiest tree in the yard. A swing, waiting for a little girl who needed a home, a mother... and a father.

"No!" Beck exclaimed. "I can't believe you did it. Taylor, I have to draw the line somewhere. You think you can come into my life and help me adopt a child, set up house, hang a tire swing—and then just step back and call it 'a little help.' Forget it! You can't have things both ways. You can't try to create a family, and then say you're not really involved. In other words, I don't want your darn tire swing in my backyard!"

"You're being unreasonable about this. Why shouldn't I step in now and then if it'll make things easier for you? It's only until you find a real father for the kid."

She strode out the back door to the tire swing and fumbled with the rope. When Taylor came after her, she turned to face him.

"I want this out of here. My life's not going to be a convenience for you any longer. You know what, Taylor? You've been using me. That's right—using me. You're determined to remain a bachelor, but around me you figure you can dabble in 'family time' when the mood hits you. I see what's going to happen if I let this go on. You'll drop by with presents for my child now and then, and you'll be pleased when she calls you 'Uncle Taylor.' Good old Uncle Taylor, popping in between baseball games, sampling what it's like to be a father and then escaping back to safety again. Well, go be Uncle Taylor somewhere else!'' She yanked on the dratted rope of the swing, making the leaves of the willow rustle all around her.

"You're blowing this all out of proportion," he said. "Can't a guy do you a favor or two without paying for it?"

She closed her eyes. "There are favors . . . and then there are favors. You're using me to taste family life without any risk. I won't let you do it."

Somehow she found herself in his arms, her cheek pressed against his shoulder. "Rebecca, you think I'm only hanging around you because you're adopting a kid? Maybe I'm popping in and out of your life because I want to see *you*."

She allowed herself one moment to relish the feel of his arms around her—one moment only. Then she pulled away.

"Maybe you do want to see me," she whispered. "Maybe your sampling of family life includes wondering what it would be like if you and I . . . if you and I were together."

"So maybe I have wondered. But that's not enough to build a whole family on! I can't give you everything you need in a husband—in a father for your kids. I wish I could, Beck. I wish like the devil I could. But won't you take what I *can* give you?"

That was tempting, indeed. To go back into Taylor's arms and tell him she'd be here whenever he wanted to show up. But she couldn't do it. It would hurt too much to have only a small part of him.

"All or nothing, McCoy. That's the way it works. If you want to be around me...it has to be everything."

He gazed at her for a long moment. Then he untied the tire from its rope, bringing it to the ground with a jounce. "You sure about this, Beck?"

"Very sure."

He didn't say anything more. He simply turned and rolled the tire down the path toward the front of the house. There went Taylor McCoy, rolling that tire out of her life.

She tried to laugh, but the laughter stuck in her throat. From here she could see Taylor heave the tire into the back of his truck. He turned, gave her a brusque wave, then climbed into his truck and drove away. Just like that, he was gone. It had been quite simple, really, cutting Taylor out of her world.

Beck wrapped her arms around her body and hugged tightly as she stared at the rope dangling from the willow tree. It was all for the best, and she knew it. If she let Taylor intrude any more into her life, she'd only get false hopes. She'd really start to believe she was the one woman who could win the confirmed bachelor. Yet Taylor had made it very clear today he wasn't for the winning.

Beck tried to laugh again, but she wasn't any more successful this time. Nothing seemed very funny right now. Nothing seemed funny at all.

CHAPTER TEN

BECK SAT on a park bench, glancing at her watch. Today, for the first time she was meeting Elizabeth—the little girl who could very well become a part of her life.

Beck was so nervous she'd hardly eaten lunch. She'd hardly eaten breakfast, for that matter. Yet so far everything was proceeding well. The social worker had visited Beck at the new house and had appeared satisfied—even though boxes were piled everywhere and Beck was only half moved in. Soon after the social worker's visit, a time and place for meeting Elizabeth had been arranged. Beck had chosen the neutral territory of this park, hoping it would help the two of them relax with each other a little. There was a small playground with a slide, swing sets and a sandbox. Maybe Elizabeth liked sandboxes. Maybe she was too old for sandboxes. What did Beck know about seven-year-olds, anyway?

She glanced at her watch again, and a total of thirty seconds had passed since the last time she'd looked. If Taylor was here, he probably would've brought along a bat and a baseball. He'd be warming up, getting ready to teach Elizabeth how to hit a few pop flies. He was good with children. At the charity promotion a few days ago, he'd had a cluster of kids around him everywhere he went, several of them pawing him with baseball mitts. Yes, if Taylor were here right now, he'd be swinging a bat, telling jokes to put Beck at ease . . .

But he *wasn't* here, and Beck reminded herself why. She had to do this alone. She needed to prove she could handle this adoption process on her own. She'd be a parent on her own; she had to get used to the idea.

At last a car drove up. A young woman climbed out, accompanied by a dark-haired child. They approached Beck, although the little girl scuffed along behind the woman.

"Ms. Danley? I'm Karen Morrow from the agency And this is Elizabeth." The woman gently pushed the little girl forward. "I'm going to leave the two of you alone for a short while, but I'll be at the other end of the park if either one of you needs me."

Almost too quickly Beck was left alone with Elizabeth. The child stood in front of her, not moving, not speaking, apparently concentrating very hard on wishing she was somewhere else. Elizabeth had serious brown eyes and bangs so straight they looked like they'd been cut with a ruler. She clutched a book under one arm the way most little girls would carry a doll.

"Hello," Beck said. "I'm Rebecca. Everybody calls me Beck, though. Do you have a nickname like me?"

"My name is Elizabeth," the child said with some dignity.

"That's fine. It's a pretty name. Why don't you sit down and we'll talk a little."

Elizabeth climbed onto the bench, just about as far away as she could get from Beck. This conversation wasn't starting very well at all. Beck was usually comfortable with the children she photographed. But it was easy to be comfortable with kids when nothing major was at stake. Today a great deal was at stake, and Beck hardly knew where to begin.

"What book is that, Elizabeth?"

"It's about a dog. I don't have a dog." Elizabeth opened her book and started turning pages intently, as if hoping Beck would disappear in the process.

"I don't have a dog, either," Beck said. "But I like dogs. I have a house now—and come to think of it, I ought to get a dog. A cocker spaniel, maybe?"

"German shepherd." Elizabeth darted a glance at Beck. For just a second she seemed almost unguarded, but then all barriers went solidly back into place. She dove inside her book again, turning pages and mouthing words silently to herself.

Maybe it was best simply to leave Elizabeth to her own devices for a moment. Beck did something she'd often found to be an icebreaker with children. Pretending to be thoroughly engrossed, she picked up her camera from its place on the bench beside her and focused on the trees in the distance. She clicked the shutter. Next she focused on a sparrow hopping nearby... click. She was careful not to pay any attention to Elizabeth, going through an elaborate ritual of screwing off her lens and replacing it with another. By this point, most kids would be poking their fingers at the camera, begging to take a picture themselves. But so far Beck hadn't sensed one iota of interest from Elizabeth. She risked a glance in the child's direction and could've sworn Elizabeth was peering at her out of the corner of her eye. Then again, maybe not. Elizabeth dipped her head closer to her book.

It was like going fishing and getting nary a bite on the line. Beck took a few more pictures, afterward resting her camera in her lap. Maybe the direct approach was best.

"Elizabeth, do you know why you're meeting me today?"

The little girl didn't glance up from her book. "You want to look me over."

Beck turned a little toward Elizabeth. "Me, I don't picture building a family like going to the grocery store. The way I see it, people keep looking, hoping to find someone special..." Beck cursed herself for being so inept, but she didn't want to push things too much. She wanted to win Elizabeth's confidence first.

Some instinct deep inside told Beck that she and Elizabeth were two people who belonged together. It was a quiet, sure conviction, not the excitement she'd expected. And she couldn't say exactly why she felt this way. Maybe it was Elizabeth's perfectly straight bangs that touched her, or maybe that book about a dog, the pages looking about to shred from being handled so much. Maybe it was the child's silence that reached Beck most of all, the silence of someone who wanted desperately to protect herself.

"Elizabeth, I think you're right. A German shepherd is a very good dog to have."

Again, almost a glance. Almost, but not quite. And now Karen Morrow was coming back across the park to claim Elizabeth. At Karen's prompting, Elizabeth said goodbye to Beck with a formality that seemed much too old for her years.

Beck walked slowly to her apartment, camera dangling from her neck. It wasn't going to be easy winning Elizabeth over. In a way it seemed rather like trying to win Taylor McCoy.

Except that Beck had given up on Taylor, and rightfully so! But she wouldn't give up on Elizabeth. If ever a little girl was meant to be with Beck, this was the one. Someday she wanted to see Elizabeth running through the house, making lots of noise and causing trouble and not being polite at all—like a seven-year-old who was confident of her parents' love. Make that *one* parent, of course.

At her apartment, Beck couldn't sit still. She needed to talk to someone about Elizabeth. She lifted the telephone receiver. Maybe her own mother... No, that wouldn't do. Her parents were worried about the step she was about to take. They wanted her to wait and think it over some more; they wouldn't understand about Elizabeth. Beck replaced the receiver and thought hard. She had several good friends, parents themselves, who supported her decision. But somehow she didn't want to talk to any of them right now. What she really wanted...darn, what she really wanted was to talk to Taylor McCoy.

She wanted to tell him everything: how pretty soon she was going to end up with not only a daughter, but a German shepherd, too. She wanted to tell him she was sure about Elizabeth, and yet worried that she wouldn't be able to reach this child's heart. It was one thing to know a child was meant for you, but how did you convince a child you were meant for her? Beck wanted to ask Taylor that very question, and she reached once again for the phone.

Then she stopped herself. She sank into a chair, cradling her head in her hands and reminding herself that she'd been the one to cut Taylor out of her life. She had no business calling him, even though it seemed the most natural thing to do.

How quickly she'd come to depend on Taylor these past few months! When she'd decided to adopt a child, he'd been the first one she'd told. In a way, she'd been asking for his help that day. And then, when he'd gone ahead and helped her, she'd turned on him and accused him of using her. Had she really been fair?

Beck rubbed her forehead, no easy answers coming. Oh, her life was a muddle!

She grabbed the phone receiver, punched out Taylor's number and sat waiting anxiously. No answer came, although she let the phone ring a very long time. He would be at the ballpark, of course. Where else?

She plunked the receiver back into place, took her camera bag and headed out the door.

SOME HOURS LATER Beck wandered through the empty stands of the stadium. Taylor was nowhere to be found. She hadn't had a chance to catch him before the game, and now he seemed to have disappeared. None of the players she'd asked knew where he was. Apparently they didn't want to be around Taylor at the moment. They'd lost the game, and they all knew how much Taylor hated to see his team lose. Manager Taylor McCoy was not a person a ball player would want to see after a rout like this afternoon's.

Beck, however, wasn't ready to give up her search. The need to talk to him was too intense. She went down the steps toward the baseball diamond. The maintenance crew was already busy, a small tractor smoothing out the infield. A few of the players lingered next to the dugout, and Beck asked if any of them had seen Taylor.

"Bet I know where he is," volunteered the catcher. "Sometimes after a bad game, he likes to head over to the batting range down the street and hit a few balls. You'll probably find him there."

"Thanks. I'll try it." She hurried off, and a few moments later she was driving up to the batting range. Dusk was falling, and only a few other cars were there. She saw Taylor's pickup right away, and she parked next to it.

She walked around the batting cages, peering through the chain-link fence. In one cage a Little Leaguer was being coached by his mother, in another a teenager was popping gum and bunting curves, and farther down, off by himself, Taylor was swinging a bat ruthlessly and methodically at the fast balls that came hurtling out of the machine.

His concentration was complete, and he seemed totally unaware of Beck standing at the other side of the fence. His face was shadowed by the batting helmet he wore, but she could see the grim lines of his profile. Again and again he swung, relentless as his bat smacked ball after ball. He seemed to be pushing himself toward some limit only he knew; this was no mere practice session. Beck stuck her fingers through the links of the fence, wanting to call to him to stop. But she remained silent, suspecting that perhaps he needed to swing that bat with all his strength, punishing the balls that shot toward him. It was only when he dropped the bat of his own accord and gripped his shoulder that she realized he'd been punishing himself, as well.

"Taylor!" she exclaimed, yanking open the gate. "What are you thinking? You'll hurt yourself even more!"

He brushed past her, going to sit on a bench. He was breathing heavily, the sweat trickling down his face, and he held his shoulder as if in a great deal of pain. But trust Taylor McCoy not to say a word about that. He swore a few times under his breath, and that was all. Beck sat down beside him. When he eased off his batting helmet, she took it from him.

"Something tells me this isn't just about losing a game," she said. "Want to talk?"

"You should leave, Beck."

She remained stubbornly beside him. "You've helped me when I needed it. Let me help you for once."

He massaged his shoulder gingerly, wincing, but he didn't answer. He seemed lost in his own thoughts. Well, Beck wasn't impatient at the moment. She could wait. She sat beside Taylor in the gathering dusk. Eventually the batting range grew deserted, no one left but the two of them. After a while Taylor propped his elbows on his knees and stared off into the distance.

"Sometimes I think I'll work beyond it," he said in a low voice. "Sometimes I think I'll come out here and hit and hit until I move beyond the injury. I try to force my shoulder to be the way it was before—only it never happens. I still end up lame, with dreams I can't go after anymore."

"Maybe it's time for you to dream new dreams. Maybe being a manager isn't so bad."

"Don't you understand what it's like? Seeing somebody else out there at home plate, missing a slider I know I could've hit ... I'm just rubbing salt in the wound, Beck! Being a manager is a mistake for me."

"Too bad you're such a natural at coaching. Inspiring the team, getting everybody to shape up after a loss. You watch. Tomorrow the Roadrunners will win, just so they don't disappoint you."

He rubbed his shoulder a little, still wincing. When he didn't answer, she went on speaking.

"When you think of it, Taylor, there's something awfully satisfying about getting *other* people to win. I mean, I do it all the time in my own line of work. Maybe I'm not out there center stage or anything, but I get the satisfaction of making things happen. It's like being the director of a movie. I'm in control, yet behind the scenes. Your job is the same. Can't you look at it that way?"

He shook his head. "I never wanted to direct somebody else's actions. Making it to the majors, that's the only thing I ever dreamed about when I was a player. The day I got drafted into the big leagues and started earning real money for the first time in my life, I thought I had it made. I got cocky as hell for a while there. And then I actually settled down and just did my job. Thought I'd finally found my place, until my shoulder gave out on me...."

"You've found another place for yourself, right here in New Mexico." Beck wanted to reach over and shake him for emphasis, but she didn't think that would do his sore shoulder any good. "Listen to me, Taylor. You remind me of a client or two I've had. People who have one dream all their lives and can't even think about anything else. Maybe they want to sing, or be a comedian—whatever, it doesn't matter. The point is, they forget about everything else but that one big goal. Maybe they succeed, maybe they don't, but they're miserable either way because everything's riding on the big dream. They don't have any perspective, any balance in their lives."

Taylor grimaced. "Is there a point to all this?"

"Yes, there is. Here's what I tell my clients. I tell them to go after their dreams with everything they've got—but I also tell them to take up a hobby."

"Is this a not-so-subtle hint I should start building model airplanes or something?"

"Wouldn't be a bad idea at all. Okay, here's an example. There's this dancer I represent, and she used to get so twisted up in knots about her career that she couldn't even go on auditions anymore. So I told her maybe she should do something in her spare time that didn't have a thing to do with dancing. I told her she ought to take up bird-watching or macramé or piano. Turned out bird-watching did the trick, Taylor. She's going on auditions again, but she doesn't fall to pieces when she loses a part. Instead, she just takes her binoculars and goes off in search of a downy woodpecker or a yellow-breasted chat."

Taylor looked highly skeptical. "There's actually some poor bird out there called a yellow-breasted chat? Anyway, I don't do hobbies."

"That's your problem right there."

"Beck, did you come here to tell me I need to take up bird-watching?"

She sighed. "No. I came because...because I've missed you, darn it. I've missed you interfering with my life. I know it doesn't make sense, but what am I supposed to do about it? Tell me that!"

"You could always try bird-watching."

She gave him a disparaging glance. "Well, at least you haven't lost your sense of humor. But something happened today, and I just wanted to share it with you. I met her, Taylor. I met Elizabeth."

Now he looked cautiously interested. "What's the verdict?"

"There wasn't a doubt in my mind from the minute I saw her. I know she and I are supposed to be part of a family together. But she's tough. She wouldn't give an inch. I've got to win her trust somehow. If only you could have seen her, Taylor! Dark brown eyes, and dark pretty hair, and I swear she's already a cynic at seven years old. The strangest thing is that she reminds me of you."

He lifted his hands. "Uh, look, Beck, I don't think you should be telling me any of this. I've been considering things, and you were right the first time. I shouldn't be worming my way into your life unless I intend to stay. It's not fair to you, and it wouldn't be fair to a kid."

Beck despised herself for her own weakness, but she succumbed to it. "I know what I told you about staying away. But maybe I was wrong. Maybe we could be friends. We were starting to become friends, weren't we?"

"We were becoming a lot more than friends, Rebecca. That's the problem."

The twilight had turned a deep lavender blue all around them. Then the lights of the batting range popped on, and dusk was replaced with the harsh glow of a thousand watts.

"Maybe we should see what happens between us," she said. "Maybe we should just—"

"No, Beck." His voice was stern. "You were right, and you shouldn't back down. Sure, you tell me I need a hobby—but you're not going to be my hobby. You deserve a lot more than that."

"I know I'm the one who started all this. I'm the one who tried to shut you out, but I can't even seem to last a week without...without seeing you. How can it be so easy for you to shut *me* out?"

He gazed at her, and now his gray eyes seemed as dark as the approaching night. "Hell, no, it's not easy," he said, his voice rough. "But I've finally figured at least one thing out. When I was a ball player, I gave the game everything I had. I didn't hold back. And somehow my life has to be like that again. Either I'm going to do something all the way, or I'm not going to do it at all." He took his batting helmet from her and put it back on. Then he went to the cage and picked up his bat.

She stood on the other side of the fence. "This is your solution? You're just going to keep hitting the damn ball forever?"

"I'll hit the ball until it breaks—or I do."

Beck turned away, her heart aching. Just now she had asked Taylor to share her life in any way he could. But he had refused her. There would be no sharing between them, after all.

She left quickly after that. She couldn't bear to stay there and watch him push his own limits so harshly.

And she couldn't bear to stay, knowing that she'd really lost him this time.

NEVER GET PERSONAL with a client. That was Beck's new motto. Too bad she hadn't come up with it the day she met Taylor! Right now she was in a very distressing situation. She'd told Taylor to stop intruding in her life—and yet that evening at the batting range she'd practically thrown herself at him. No question about it; she'd thrown herself at the confirmed bachelor. He'd rejected her of course, and instead of being able to retreat and nurse her wounds with a little dignity, Beck had to go on publicizing the team—and that meant publicizing the confirmed bachelor. Yes, it was very distressing.

Beck stood outside the door to Taylor's office, wondering how on earth she was going to handle seeing him again. She'd managed to avoid the ballpark the past couple of days, concentrating on her other clients, instead. But working with Taylor was inevitable; she had to keep doing a good job for the Roadrunners. So here she was, back at the stadium.

She gritted her teeth. Then she raised her fist and knocked on his door.

"Come in!"

Still gritting her teeth, Beck swung the door open and wheeled a dolly loaded with boxes into Taylor's cluttered office. He was standing at one of the charts tacked to the wall, scribbling away. He didn't turn around.

"That you, Vince?" he asked. "We need to talk about the starting lineup. I want to make some changes."

Beck cleared her throat. "Hello, Taylor. It's me."

Now he did turn around. "Uh...hello there." As she pushed the dolly toward him, he looked at her as if she were delivering a load of skunks.

"Don't worry, this is job-related," she said briskly, stopping to open one of the boxes. "I have the special programs ready for you to sign."

He scanned the stack of boxes. "You've got to be kidding. Get somebody else to sign them. Stan Parker's popular with the fans right now."

"Stan's a good hitter, all right, but people want *your* autograph, Taylor. You're the star of the team, whether you like it or not." She carried a stack of the special-edition programs to his desk. "If you don't mind, we'll get started. I need a batch of these for the game tonight. Now that you're in the playoffs, I really expect the programs to sell."

Beck cleared a couple of baseball mitts off a chair and sat down. So far, so good. She was handling this encounter well; she was getting on with business. A little cooperation from Taylor, and she'd be out of here before either of them knew it.

He sat down at his desk with some reluctance and opened the first program. "Okay, okay, where do I sign?"

Beck consulted the sheet she'd written up. "Page forty-nine, please, above the ad for Benny's Hot Dogs. The lucky fan who ends up with this program wins two free foot-longs."

Taylor jotted his signature, then flipped through some of the other pages. "Not a bad layout. You design this yourself, Beck?"

"Yes, I did." She was rather proud of the program and leaned forward to point out the highlights. "Here's an interview with the organist. Nobody ever gets to see the organist, and people want to know who plays all that wonderful music at the games. And over here, I've included a bio on each player…" Her voice trailed off. Taylor was studying her, yet he didn't seem to be listening to a word she was saying. She wondered what he was thinking. "Anyway, there's a bio on you, too. I think you'll be happy with it. I didn't get too personal or anything."

"Damn, another picture of me—with a tie on this time."

Beck thought it was one of the best photos she'd taken of him. It showed him standing at home plate in a dark suit, resting the tip of a bat against the ground. He was staring off into the distance as he often did, a yearning on his face that seemed to capture the spirit of baseball.

Taylor read the short biography under the photo. "You've got all my career stats here, but no hobbies listed. I'm surprised you didn't invent one or two for me. You could've told people I was a bird-watcher."

"I'm through trying to reform your character." Beck's attempt at a lighthearted tone failed, and she hurried on. "Next program—sign page four, please, under the Can-a-Corn ad. This signature will be worth a tub of popcorn."

For a while Taylor went on signing programs, but then he stopped. "Believe it or not, I've been thinking about what you said. Hobbies, that kind of thing."

"Glad to hear it. Page twenty-two, by the picture of the sea lion, if you don't mind. This is an important one—worth a free trip to the zoo."

"Beck, I've always liked horses, and lately I've been picturing myself on a ranch. A horse ranch. Plenty of room in New Mexico for that."

"You're talking some hobby," she murmured. "An entire ranch."

"Why start small? I've got the money to invest in a good-size spread. I could hire a few hands, maybe take riding more seriously. I might make a pretty damn good roper."

Beck could see his tantalizing vision: horses like Davy roaming over miles of sagebrush beneath the blue New Mexico sky, Taylor in dusty jeans, carrying a saddle and looking contented . . .

"It sounds great. Go for it, Taylor."

"Yeah, well, it's just an idea right now. I'm playing around with it, seeing where it takes me."

"I'm happy for you."

They stared at each other. It took Beck a minute to remember what she was supposed to be doing. She slid another program in front of him.

"Um . . . page nineteen."

"Beck, how's it going with you? What's the news with Elizabeth?"

"Last time you didn't want to hear about it."

"I wanted to hear. I just didn't want to get too involved."

"So we'll keep it that way," she said tightly. "Page nineteen."

He frowned at the program in front of him. "Dammit, Beck, tell me what's going on. It doesn't mean I'll start barging into your life again. But I can't help being interested in you, all right? Adopting that kid on your own—I can't stop thinking about it.''

"I'm meant to be Elizabeth's mother. Nothing else matters."

"Wrong, Beck. A whole lot else matters. It's written all over your face. You've still got the order of things mixed up. In spite of everything, you're still waiting for romance.''

CHAPTER ELEVEN

BECK DIDN'T WANT to wait around to hear anything else. She gathered up the programs Taylor had already signed. "These will have to do for now. This just doesn't seem like the greatest time for a business meeting. We'll try again later."

"Ignoring the problem isn't going to make it go away."

"I don't have a problem."

"Sure you do. And I hold myself partly responsible. I didn't do a good enough job of helping you find a man."

She didn't like the glint in his eye. "If you're thinking of starting all *that* over again, you'd better think twice. No more dating services. No more introductions to total strangers on airplanes!"

"You need romance, Beck. You need it bad."

He'd goaded her too far. She clutched her programs in a jumbled pile and somehow found herself blurting out everything she'd meant to keep hidden.

"You're entirely mistaken, Taylor. I'm not waiting around for romance. I already seem to have found it— in the most inconvenient place possible. Unfortunately I seem to have found it with you! The trouble is, you haven't found it with *me*. Are you happy now? Did you want to hear the whole sorry mess?"

Taylor looked as pained as if she'd just slugged his bad shoulder. "Damn, I was afraid of this. I was afraid we'd already taken things too far."

"No, I'm the one who's gone too far. You'll never go too far because you're so all-fired determined to stay safe and be a confirmed bachelor. Well, there's nothing safe about my life anymore. I've jumped right over the cliff!" She was really losing it. She was throwing herself at Taylor again. She had to get out of here before she made things even worse. She strode to the door, one or two programs sliding unheeded out of her arms and flapping to the ground.

"Beck, I think we'd better talk this out."

She was beyond talking things out—but apparently she wasn't beyond making things worse. She paused at the door and gazed at Taylor. Now she said the rest of it, revealing all her pain and longing to him.

"The truth is, I seem to be falling in love with you. And if you haven't figured that out by now, talking's not going to do either one of us a bit of good."

THE LAST GAME of the season was under way, and the stadium was packed to overflowing. This afternoon would decide whether the Roadrunners won the league pennant or went down in defeat. For Taylor's sake, Beck hoped fervently that his team would win. It didn't seem fair that all his work, all his coaching, had to come down to this single game. But that was the way it was in sports—only one winner allowed in the end. And Taylor seemed to thrive on the intense competition. He was down on the field now, sending signals to his players, pacing in front of the dugout, occasionally waving his arms as he yelled at the umpire.

Beck smiled a little, watching the game from the glass-enclosed owner's box high up in the stadium. Elizabeth stood beside her, and Beck glanced over at the little girl. Today Elizabeth wore a Roadrunners T-shirt and a baseball cap that was a shade too big for her. She also carried a baseball mitt, purchased downstairs at the souvenir stand. Elizabeth didn't look quite at home in all her baseball paraphernalia; every so often she examined her mitt as if wondering how she'd come to possess such a device. Beck smiled ruefully now, realizing she'd gotten carried away while outfitting Elizabeth for the game.

The baseball cap sat at a precise angle on Elizabeth's head, above the perfectly straight line of her bangs. In Beck's many visits with Elizabeth of late, she'd learned that the girl craved precision in her life; perhaps it was the only way she could deal with the uncertainty she'd already experienced. Beck reached over and took hold of Elizabeth's hand. Elizabeth gave her a solemn look, then pressed her nose against the glass to watch more of the game.

Beck and Elizabeth stood a little apart from the others milling about in the owner's box. Alma Latham had invited a small group to share this last game of the season with her. Since Alma knew about Beck's plans to adopt, she'd included a special invitation for Elizabeth. So far it was impossible to tell if Elizabeth was enjoying herself. The little girl behaved in her usual polite manner, giving no hint of her feelings. At the moment she looked much too small in her oversize T-shirt and her oversize cap. Beck longed to gather the child up in her arms and give her a hug, but her intuition still warned her to go slow with Elizabeth. According to the agency, it was only a matter of time before the adoption would be finalized; meanwhile, Beck visited with Elizabeth as often as possible and did everything she could to gain the little girl's trust. Was she succeeding? With all her heart, she hoped so.

Beck turned again to watch the field. It was a close game so far, the Roadrunners ahead by only one run in the third inning. Even from here, Beck could feel the tension radiating from Taylor. He strode back and forth behind the baseline, looking lean and powerful in his sea-blue uniform, the number 22 emblazoned in burgundy on the back of his jersey. It was Taylor's lucky number. He'd worn it as a player in the majors, and it had seen him to a World Series victory. Hopefully 22 was still a lucky number and would see the Roadrunners to victory.

By now Beck had become thoroughly swept up in all the delightful superstitions of baseball. In fact, baseball in general was a big part of her life these days, and she wondered how she was going to handle the off-season. Beck gazed down at Taylor, a heavy ache inside her. She didn't know how she was going to handle the off-season without *him*. He'd seemed awfully troubled the day she'd admitted she was falling in love with him. He'd even tried to talk her out of it. She remembered every single word he'd said: "Beck, you can't really be in love with me. Once you find the right guy, you'll forget all about me. Trust me, that's the way it'll happen."

Beck knew it wouldn't do any good to argue that Taylor himself was the right guy. If he didn't believe it, none of her own convictions mattered. So why did her contrary heart still insist that Taylor McCoy was the right man for her?

Beck was drawn from her wistful reverie by the sound of Alma Latham's voice behind her.

"Rebecca, Elizabeth, I thought you'd like to meet my granddaughter. This is Cassie."

Cassie was an energetic nine-year-old who immediately took matters in her own hands. "C'mon," she said, dragging Elizabeth off with her. "My grandma has the best collection of baseball cards you ever saw, I'll show you."

Elizabeth craned her head around to look at Beck. She seemed uncertain, and Beck was severely tempted to run after her and rescue her from Cassie.

"They'll be fine," Alma said at Beck's elbow as if reading her thoughts. "All new mothers worry too much, you know. It comes with the territory."

"She hasn't even moved in with me yet, and already I'm awake nights wondering how I'll handle her teenage years. You're telling me this is normal?"

"Perfectly normal," Alma said cheerfully. "If you want to know the truth, I still worry about my thirty-year-old son who has a new girlfriend every six months. I swear, every time he changes the spark plugs on his car he has a different fiancée. Sorry, Rebecca, but you can look forward to a whole lifetime of this."

Somehow Beck didn't mind. Part of life was having somebody to worry about, somebody to love. But there wasn't time to think about it; Alma was leading her off to a corner for an impromptu business meeting. Alma shared her granddaughter's energy and decisive personality. She was sixty-two but possessed all the enthusiasm of a kid—surely a requirement for anyone who was enthralled with baseball.

Now Alma settled Beck into a seat beside her where they could both see the game. Alma wore a custom-made jersey in the new team colors of blue and burgundy. She fished in a pocket of the jersey, pulled out an envelope and handed it to Beck.

"Your bonus," she announced. "You earned every penny, Rebecca. Attendance has skyrocketed since you came on board. I hope you'll be back with us next season."

Beck fingered the envelope. "I'd like that very much. But I can't take all the credit for the sellout crowds. It's Taylor. He has something special that draws people."

Alma grinned. "You mean he's one gorgeous hunk of male, and every woman in the state wants to get her hands on him. But you're the one who publicized him as the confirmed bachelor. Take the credit you deserve."

Beck gazed out at the field, still hurting inside. "Maybe it wasn't the best campaign, promoting Taylor that way. It seems to have gotten . . . out of control."

Alma looked sympathetic and reached over to pat Beck's hand. "Okay, so you fell for him, too, along with all the other ladies. But you just hang in there. Taylor will come around. He'll realize how much he needs you."

Beck gave the older woman a startled glance. "It doesn't show that much, does it? The way I feel about him?"

"Of course it shows. And my ball players are placing bets on how long it'll take Taylor to come to his senses and propose to you. Now, Rebecca, don't interpret this as pressure, but my bet says he'll do it by Halloween. October thirty-first, and not a day later."

The situation was even worse than Beck had imagined! The entire team knew she'd fallen for her own publicity campaign. She might as well wear a sign on her head that said, "I'm yours, Taylor McCoy." What was she going to do?

For the moment there was no choice but to watch the game. Stan Parker came up to bat and hit a homer that put the Roadrunners ahead by two. The crowd went wild, and every single person in the owner's box let out a cheer. Beck cheered, too, jumping out of her seat. Down on the field, Taylor slapped his cap against his leg in a gesture of triumph, then promptly put his cap back on and folded his arms sternly over his chest. Taylor was not one to get cocky before the game was over. It was only the bottom of the fifth.

The organist played a medley of show tunes, a teenage vendor popped his head into the owner's box to see if anybody wanted more peanuts, and the announcer proclaimed over the loudspeaker that whoever had Taylor's signature on page thirty-five of the program—next to the ad for the All-Points Travel Agency—had just won a trip to Santa Fe. Then Cassie reappeared, still dragging Elizabeth along. Elizabeth's cap no longer sat straight, but was slightly askew. She looked rather happy to have found a friend.

Cassie stood by the window and cheered on her grandmother's team. "Sweep 'em out of the stadium!

Aw, c'mon, shouldda been a double. What's with Ernie today?''

"C'mon, Ernie, shouldda been a double," Elizabeth echoed in a small voice. This time she was the one who slipped her hand into Beck's. "I want to come here again," she said. "Can we, Mom? Can we?"

For a second Beck almost didn't dare to breathe. How naturally that word had come from Elizabeth: Mom. She probably didn't even realize she'd said it, but there it was, an unexpected gift for Beck. A wonderful gift.

Beck squeezed Elizabeth's fingers in her own. "Next season it's you and me at every game. You can help me with my work. In fact, you can help me right now. I need to go take some pictures, and I'd sure like somebody to carry my camera bag."

Together Beck and Elizabeth made their way down through the crowded stands. Elizabeth had the camera bag slung around her neck, and now she definitely looked happy. She stopped for a moment, gazing intently at Beck.

"I need a nickname," she said. "Just like you."

Beck smiled at her new daughter. "I'm sure we'll be able to come up with just the right nickname. What do you think of Beth? That's pretty."

Elizabeth looked thoughtful, and then she nodded. She gave a quick shy smile. "Beth is good. It sounds like Beck." With that she went on skipping down through the stands.

Beck followed, treasuring a happiness all her own. And yet, at the same time, she still had that deep ache inside that wouldn't go away. She was making such a good start on a family—but it wasn't a complete family. Someone very important was missing.

Beck took some pictures of the players on the field, using her zoom lens, but she needed to get some closer shots, too. By the time the seventh-inning stretch came around, she and Elizabeth were working near the Roadrunners' dugout. Taylor approached as soon as he caught sight of them.

Beck could feel her heart pounding. Right now she was going to introduce two people who mattered very much to her, and it was impossible to be casual about it. She almost dropped her camera on her toe.

"Elizabeth—Beth—this is Mr. McCoy. Taylor McCoy, actually, team manager."

Taylor gave Beck a quick glance, as if to gauge whether she was foolish enough today to be in love with him. She tried to act as if she didn't have the least interest in a bachelor of his qualifications. She suspected, however, that she wasn't being very successful at feigning disinterest.

Now Taylor took the little girl's hand in a gentle grip and shook it solemnly. "Elizabeth, I've been hoping I'd get to meet you. How are you enjoying the game so far?"

Elizabeth clung to Beck's side. "It's fine, thank you."

"That's a pretty good mitt you have there. Regulation-size and everything. You must play with the majors."

Elizabeth shook her head silently. Taylor squatted down beside her.

"You know, I wouldn't mind teaching you how to field a ball. In fact, you come out here to the stadium sometime, and we'll take some batting practice. Sound like fun?"

She nodded, giving Taylor one of her elusive smiles. Beck wanted to protest, and she frowned at Taylor. Damn, it wasn't fair for him to make Elizabeth an offer he couldn't follow through on. He'd already said he wouldn't do anything by half measure; he'd said he wouldn't give a child of Beck's any false hopes.

As if sensing Beck's discomfort, he straightened up and gave her an apologetic shrug. It didn't make her feel any better.

"I'm going to get a dog," Elizabeth said. "Me and Beck, we're going to get a dog. A German shepherd."

"Is that so? Sounds like an excellent choice to me. I've always liked German shepherds, myself... Sorry Elizabeth, gotta get back to the game now. Talk to you later, okay?"

"Okay."

Taylor gazed intently at Beck, perhaps wanting to say something to her. But his third-base coach was gesturing for a consultation, so he strode away, immersed in baseball once more.

Beck found it difficult to concentrate on her job after that. She knew she ought to be taking pictures of the players, but more often than not her camera swung between Taylor McCoy and Elizabeth. She captured Elizabeth waving her mitt in the air after one of the Roadrunners made a hit. She captured Taylor as he made his mysterious signals: hand to his elbow, finger tipped to his cap, fist thumped against his chest. Beck knew what she really wanted was a picture of him and Elizabeth together. It just seemed somehow that he and Elizabeth belonged with each other. Both of them were just a little too cynical about love, and they both needed someone to show them love was entirely possible....

Stop! Beck commanded herself fiercely. She was only increasing her torment. This was the last game of the season. After today, Taylor would be gone from her life. Maybe he'd take that job as scout for the majors, or maybe he'd set off to buy a ranch somewhere. Either way, he'd be gone, and Beck would be starting her own new life with Elizabeth.

Meanwhile, the ninth inning wasn't looking good. The other team, with only one out, knocked in two runs, tying the score. Taylor prowled the baseline, cap jammed low over his forehead. The pitcher stood on the mound, head bent in concentration. Then came his windup—and the batter made a base hit, driving in another run. Now the Roadrunners were lagging by one.

Beck had taken Elizabeth behind the safety net at home plate. She snapped photos as Taylor went out to the mound. He stood in deep conversation with the pitcher for a moment, then clapped the man on the shoulder and strode back toward the dugout. Whatever he said apparently did the job, for shortly afterward the pitcher struck out two batters. But the Roadrunners were still behind, and it was the bottom of the ninth.

The organist played a marching tune and the fans yelled encouragement from the stands, but it didn't look promising, not promising at all. Elizabeth handed Beck a new roll of film.

"We gonna win, Beck?"

It would probably take Elizabeth a little while to get used to saying "Mom" all the time, but Beck wasn't in a hurry. She smiled at her daughter again.

"I sure hope we win. Send all your good thoughts to Mr. McCoy and maybe that'll help."

Beck wished she hadn't mentioned Taylor's name. In the future she'd have to watch this tendency to talk about him. But right now she sent all her own good thoughts toward him right along with Elizabeth's. She wanted the Roadrunners to win for his sake.

The leadoff man made it to first, but the second batter struck out. So did the next. Bottom of the ninth and two outs—not good. Now Stan Parker was up to bat. "Stan! Stan! Stan!" chanted the crowd. He gripped the bat, hunched over the plate—and hit the ball clear out of the park. The man on first sailed home, and so did Stan. The Roadrunners had won the pennant.

The fans went wild. They ran out onto the field, hugging players, hugging each other. The organ music crescendoed, but was almost lost in the cheers of the crowd. Taylor was swept away with the other players, and Beck didn't have a chance to congratulate him. She stayed with Elizabeth behind the net, waiting for some of the mayhem to die down. But she needed to see Taylor McCoy one last time, and after a while she led Elizabeth down to the players' clubhouse.

The celebration inside was going strong. Just about every player was soaked with champagne. Light bulbs flashed as newspaper photographers got to work, and one of the local TV stations had a camera set up. Beck put the lens cap on her own camera, deciding she'd taken enough pictures. Alma Latham, looking resplendent in her blue and burgundy baseball jersey, was giving an interview to a magazine reporter. Cassie, Jenny the batgirl and several other kids were running around, and they immediately recruited Elizabeth. This time Elizabeth didn't look back as she went off to join her new friends; she was starting to act like a real seven-year-old.

Soon Taylor appeared at Beck's side. He'd showered and changed from his champagne-soaked uniform into khaki slacks and a blue cotton shirt. His hair was curling damply, and he looked fresh and vibrant, still exultant with victory. But he steered Beck toward the door.

"Let's get out of here before these press people drive me crazy," he said. Together he and Beck escaped to an isolated corner of the field.

A few diehard fans were scooping up chunks of sod and carrying them away like trophies. In proper baseball tradition, even the stuffed canvas bags that marked the bases had been ferried off by triumphant fans. No one minded; after all, it was the only way to show the correct enthusiasm for winning the pennant. The children spilled out onto the baseball diamond now. Elizabeth waved at Beck, her cap tilted crookedly by this time and in danger of flying off her head. Even her perfectly straight bangs were starting to get mussed. Beck waved back at her. The two of them were going to be okay together, no matter what happened.

Beck turned to Taylor, and suddenly she didn't know quite what to say.

"Congratulations," she offered at last. "You must be awfully pleased."

He pushed the damp hair away from his forehead. "There's nothing like winning, Beck. I'm damn pleased."

"Well, and . . . I'm pleased for you. Very pleased." She figured if either one of them sounded any more pleased, they'd be in serious trouble. If only she could say what was really in her heart and know that Taylor would listen.

Just then Elizabeth darted over to them. "Jenny says I run fast," she informed Beck and Taylor excitedly. "She says baseball players need to run fast. Are you really gonna show me how to play baseball, Mr. McCoy?"

"You bet I am."

Elizabeth darted off again, apparently satisfied. Taylor gazed after her.

"She seems like a great kid."

"She is. The best. I'm never going to be sorry I did this—starting a family on my own." She spoke defiantly, but he only nodded.

"Sometimes I guess things just happen for the best," he said. "Even when they're out of order."

"That's right."

"Beck, when I offered to teach Elizabeth to play ball, I didn't think about—"

"About the problems it could cause," she finished for him. "We have to talk about that. I don't know what your plans are—I don't know if you'll be back with the team next season. But Elizabeth and I will be here. You should know that. And I don't want her to depend on you for things you can't . . . deliver."

"If I thought things could work out between you and me, Beck, it'd be different."

"Why don't you just say it? You're not in love with me, Taylor. And that's the only thing that really matters. If you loved me, you'd know we *could* work everything out." Beck didn't look at him. Much to her own dismay, she realized she was making a last-ditch effort to win the confirmed bachelor. She was forcing him to decide whether or not he loved her, hoping against hope he'd decide in her favor.

"Listen, Beck, it's my career that's the problem," he said in a low voice. "I still don't know what the hell I'm going to do about it. Until then . . ."

"Just say it. No more excuses. Tell me you don't love me, and we'll be done with it. We'll have . . . closure."

"You make us sound like a business deal that went bad."

"Dammit, Taylor! Just say it."

He swore under his breath, but for a long moment he didn't say anything else. He said neither the words she longed to hear nor the words she dreaded. He simply stared at the children playing on the field. And then at last he spoke.

"Beck . . . all right, you win. I'll say the damn words. I don't love you."

Beck pressed her arms tightly against her body, as if that would somehow contain all the hurt inside her. She hadn't known that actually hearing the words would cause her so much pain. She'd needed a resolution from Taylor, had demanded it of him, but if he thought this was her idea of winning, he was very mistaken.

And yet she was already proving her ability to survive. In spite of this heartbreak, she was still standing, still breathing, still going through normal everyday motions. She reached into her camera bag, took out her checkbook and quickly began jotting in it. A second later she tore off a check and handed it to him.

"Alma gave me my bonus today," she said, surprised at how steady her voice was. "I'll deposit it first thing Monday morning, and then you can cash this check. It's the down payment on the house. The season's over. Everything's over."

He made as if to crumple the check. "I don't want this. At least let me make some contribution—"

"Cash the check, Taylor. And then we'll really be finished. It'll be a relief for both of us." She went to collect Elizabeth, finding that her legs functioned quite well. It was truly amazing how someone could say something you were sure would shatter you, and the very next minute you were going on with your life. At least, you appeared to be going on with your life.

Beck didn't look back at Taylor, but all the way across the field his words seemed to echo after her: "I don't love you . . . I don't love you."

CHAPTER TWELVE

BECK PUSHED her heavy sofa across the room for what seemed like the tenth time, thoroughly out of breath. She wanted to find just the perfect spot for the thing. In fact, she wanted to find the perfect spot for everything in her new house. She stood back and surveyed the sofa critically. It appeared more inviting over here, that much was for sure. And it would allow a larger area for Elizabeth to play and spread out her toys. Beck enjoyed the thought of a great many toys underfoot. Already she'd ensconced the rocking horse in a corner of the living room. True, Elizabeth was a bit too old for a rocking horse, but someday Beck hoped to adopt a little brother or sister for Elizabeth. She was determined to create a real family, whether or not she ever found the right man to help her. Of course, in Taylor McCoy she'd almost believed she'd found the right man—the perfect man who didn't know he was perfect for her.

She sank onto the sofa and propped her feet on the coffee table. She was grateful for the rest; she'd spent the entire day trying to get the house organized. Next week the adoption would be finalized, and at last she'd be able to bring Elizabeth home with her for good. The thought cheered her. It kept her from brooding too much about Taylor McCoy.

There she went again, allowing his name to pop into her mind. And with his name came longing. The past few weeks she'd been fighting her yearnings for Taylor, but so far she hadn't done a very good job.

She straightened, swinging her feet to the floor. Somehow she had to get over him! She had to stop being in love with the confirmed bachelor, that was all there was to it. He'd made it very clear he didn't love her.

She jumped up from the sofa and began to haul her armchair into a new position. Moving furniture seemed therapeutic. It helped to keep her thoughts off Taylor at least a little. Okay, push the chair over there by the window, put the end table next to it—No, the chair had to go back. Maybe the sofa would look better under the window.... Unfortunately, it was the same sofa on which she and Taylor had settled down to watch *It Happened One Night*....

Beck worked harder. If she had to move furniture ten hours a day to forget Taylor McCoy, then she'd do it. Maybe she was a romantic, but she refused to be a martyr. She would not spend her life hurting over a man who didn't want her. She wouldn't pine for him. She wouldn't mope!

Beck got the sofa halfway to the window and then collapsed back onto the cushions. Unfortunately she couldn't deny that she *had* been moping. And pining for Taylor, and hurting over him, and all the rest of it. She couldn't seem to get him out of her mind or her heart. For once in her life she'd run a publicity campaign that had been too successful. Only now did she realize what she'd been telling New Mexico women with her campaign: ''Yes, Taylor McCoy's a confirmed bachelor, ladies, but the right woman can change his mind. The right woman can show him that marriage is something he'd actually enjoy. The fault's not really in Taylor, girls! We're the ones who have to convince him what's missing in his life. It's all up to us."

Beck was angry with herself. That was the message she'd been proclaiming, all right, underneath the photos of Taylor, underneath the stories about his vibrancy and his passion for baseball. And she'd believed the message. She'd believed, deep down, that *she'd* be the one to change Taylor, to win him over. She'd be the one to model him into her idealized version of a husband and father for her children.

Taylor himself had said it: she idealized family life. She wanted the greeting-card version, with mom and dad and happy kids. And even now she still longed for that version of family life. When she yearned for Taylor, she imagined him smack in the middle of a cozy family group with her. She imagined him with her and Elizabeth, and a whole slew of children. Oh, she was pathetic. Still dreaming that she could wave a magic wand and transform the confirmed bachelor into her dream man!

Beck jumped to her feet again. These uncomfortable revelations called for some very serious furniture moving. She was right in the middle of hauling the sofa back toward the center of the room when the doorbell rang. She went to answer it. As if she'd conjured him with her restless thoughts, Taylor McCoy stood on the front porch, balancing several mismatched paper bags in his arms. Her heart pounded at the sight of him, and she had to struggle against the swirl of her emotions.

"What do you want?" she demanded. "I'm not in the mood to talk to you right now."

"You'd better let me in, Beck. I'm going to drop this stuff any minute."

She stared at him through the screen. He did look as if he was about to drop everything. Too bad. She was sorely tempted to shut the door in his face. What did he want, anyway? He'd already told her he didn't love her. There was nothing more to talk about.

Beck gave in to temptation and swung the door shut. It was a satisfying thing to do—and, as far as she was concerned, the first positive sign that she wasn't going to pine for Taylor the rest of her life.

Thumping noises came from the other side of the door, along with some muttered oaths. It sounded as if Taylor had, indeed, dropped a few of his bags.

"Good night, Taylor," she called. "Don't come back."

"Dammit, Beck, at least let me show you what I brought."

"No chance," she said, relishing her newfound fortitude. But she did have a few things he ought to hear, and by way of compromise she went to crank open one of her old-fashioned windows. The glass swung outward inch by inch. She waited a second for Taylor to appear on the other side, and then she let him have it.

"The truth hit me tonight. Half the women in New Mexico have been wanting to change you. I wanted to change you. But now I finally realize how foolish that is. If you intend to be a bachelor, that's your problem and nobody else's. I'm not going to chase the idealized version of things anymore. And I'm sure not going to idealize *you*. Good night!''

She started cranking the window shut again, but the handle was rusty and had a tendency to stick. Taylor got a chance to poke his hand inside, waving a tin in front of her face.

"Oysters," he announced. "Smoked oysters, Beck. Doesn't that mean anything to you?"

"Not a thing." She jiggled the stubborn window handle, inwardly cursing it.

"Rebecca, this is a five-course dinner I have out here." He held up boxes of Chinese carryout. "Not just any dinner, by the way. This is a special-formula meal calculated to soften even the most resolved bachelorette."

"Very funny. In case you've forgotten, you said you don't love me. I have a good memory for that type of remark."

Taylor peered in at her. "I knew it might be a problem, what I, uh, said that day. You've got to hear me out on this. I was trying to be honest with you...."

"Wonderful. You get points for sincerity." She glared at his boxes of Chinese food. "Now you can take your wontons and go."

Taylor bent down and she heard him rustling through the sacks. A moment later he appeared again, this time proudly displaying salad from the deli. "The point is, I told you I didn't love you because I was determined not to make promises I couldn't keep."

"Fine." Beck tried to close the window again.

"You've got to hear me out." He sounded earnest, intense, as if this was a matter of great importance to him. Beck was starting to waver. She leaned against the windowsill.

"Go on, then. I'm listening."

He gazed at her, his eyes dark. "Beck, actually saying the words, actually telling you I didn't love you—that bothered the hell out of me. I kept trying to convince myself afterward that I'd done the right thing, but then I realized maybe I hadn't been so honest with you, after all."

Hope surged through her, but she fought it. Could she really dare to hope? Meanwhile, Taylor juggled his deli salad and his Chinese carryout.

"It'd sure help if you'd let me in," he said.

She hesitated. "I'm willing to hear what you have to say, Taylor. But I figure you can tell me just as well from out there. I mean, if I let you in...it wouldn't be a good idea." She didn't mention that if she opened the door to him, she'd be liable to run straight into his arms—forget the deli salad, forget everything else.

"This is what happened, Beck," he said, his voice still intense. "After we won the pennant, the guys and I went out to celebrate. Only I couldn't seem to get in the mood, and they kept asking me what was wrong. The conversation naturally turned to you, and everybody on the team had an opinion. Everybody told me I was a damn fool not to marry you on the spot. And pretty soon after that...I started to realize maybe I really was a damn fool."

Now it was disappointment that swept over Beck. He made it sound as if he was here tonight only because the team had suggested it.

She gripped the handle of the window again. "Taylor, did you ever stop to wonder why the team was so all-fired interested in your romantic status?"

"They're my buddies...."

"Right. And every single one of them has a bet on when you'll propose to me. Even Alma has a bet. She says you'll do it before Halloween."

He scowled. "Hmm, and I thought it was just team camaraderie."

"Don't propose to me on account of the Roadrunners. Face it, Taylor. You really are a confirmed bachelor. Don't let anybody tell you otherwise. Be true to your principles. Good night!"

At last she got the dratted window shut again and she sped back to the sofa. She was in a dreadful turmoil. How could she ever know what Taylor really felt for her? One minute he said he didn't love her, and the next he was outside her window with the collective team blessing behind him! What good would any of that do her?

He tapped on the window. When she didn't answer, he tapped again, a little louder this time. Well, she still had a few things to say to him. She marched back to the window and, after a concerted struggle with the handle, managed to open it a crack.

"When it comes right down to it, Taylor McCoy, I did everything I knew how to win you over. But you refused to be won, and I decided I was finished with you. That's the way I want it to be, from now on."

"This time it's me trying to win *you,* but you're sure not making it easy." He held up a can of soup and a packet of pudding. "Okay, okay, so it's not homemade, and it's not chocolate mousse. But I love you, anyway, Beck. If my players were smart enough to know that before I did, why blame them? Just give the guys credit for having some brains. Beck... I do love you." His voice was husky.

I love you. It was amazing how that simple combination of words could make all Beck's resistance vanish. She blinked a few times, telling herself she was a sentimental idiot for crying. But she was a romantic, after all, and she could hardly think of anything more romantic than Taylor McCoy waving a can of soup in her face and telling her that he loved her. A second later she opened the door and she was in his arms, and the can of soup rolled unheeded along the porch.

Taylor kissed her as if he never meant to stop. But when he did stop, he still held her close, his mouth brushing her cheek. "Beck, can you forgive me? I was so wrapped up in my own problems, I didn't recognize love when it came to me. I didn't recognize you as the one I loved."

"I suppose that sort of thing is bound to happen with a confirmed bachelor," she murmured, lacing her hands behind his neck and drawing him closer still. "You'll just have to make up for lost time, Taylor McCoy. I figured out I loved *you* quite a while ago...."

Kissing was fine. It was so wonderful, in fact, Beck forgot all about the five-course meal Taylor had brought. He, too, seemed to forget about anything but kissing her. Eventually they ended up nestled together on the sofa. Taylor drew Beck into the circle of his arms and smiled at her.

"This was all a scientific experiment," he said. "Tell me if it worked. Have I cured you of doubting me?"

She sighed and settled her head against his shoulder. "All you had to do was say you love me. That did the trick."

"Then I'll say it one more time. I love you, Beck."

Those words truly did work wonders. It was several kisses later when Taylor spoke again.

"Beck, I haven't been the best person to be around since I left the majors. I was so damn angry at myself for losing my dream, then you came along and showed me I could have other dreams. It just took me a while to listen to you. I'd convinced myself there wasn't any room for a woman in my moooed up life."

"Oh, I resisted you, too," she murmured. "For a little while at least. I refused to admit I'd actually met the man who could live up to all my romantic standards. Of course, when I did admit it, you turned out to be a tough prospect. Very tough."

He ran his fingers over her cheek. "Like it or not, you've cured me of bachelorhood. No other woman could have done it. But that leaves a small problem. Next season you'll have to find a new publicity campaign for the Roadrunners. You can't be trying to raffle off your own husband."

Beck grinned. She still couldn't believe that Taylor McCoy, the confirmed bachelor, was going to be her husband.

"You were right," he went on. "I can't turn my back on baseball. I love the game too much. I've realized it's always going to hurt, Beck, knowing I can't play. But I'm finding out I can learn to live with that. I can learn to enjoy other dreams—our dreams. Here's a beginning. The first thing you and I are going to do with Elizabeth is go look for a German shepherd pup.

Every family needs a good German shepherd, don't you think?''

She loved hearing Taylor talk about their family; nothing had ever sounded so right. A family made up of a mom and a dad, children and a dog. "I do tend to idealize things," she told him. "I don't know if I'll ever stop thinking our family *is* ideal."

"We'll make plenty of mistakes, I'm sure, just like our own parents did. But with any luck our kids will forgive us. We'll love them, and that's the most important thing. No, there's something even more important. You and I will love each other, Beck."

"I can't ask for anything more ideal than that." She was easily distracted by the taste of his lips, but then she remembered something. "Wait a minute. What about Davy? I love this house, but we can't very well have a horse galloping around our backyard."

"I've been looking to find a ranch I like. Think I've found the place, up near Santa Fe. It's perfect for Davy, and for a lot of other horses, too. That way we can live in Albuquerque, right here in this house of ours, but we can also take Elizabeth up to the ranch, teach her how to ride. It's going to be a busy life. Parenthood and baseball, ranching and public relations, all rolled up into one. Think we'll be able to handle it?"

"We'll work out the details. We'll make sure everything gets the proper attention. After all, the key is to do things in the right order. I've known that all along. I just got everything mixed up for a while."

"We'd better hurry up and get married, then. That'll still give you a chance to put things in order."

"As far as I'm concerned, they're already in perfect order," she told him. "You know, I even have the first photo for our McCoy family album. Guess I can finally get it developed, that picture of you kissing me."

"I like the real thing better." He bent his head toward her, then stopped himself. "Hold on! I've forgotten the most important part of the formula." He rattled through one of the sacks he'd brought along and pulled out a videotape. A few seconds later *It Happened One Night* flickered to life on the television screen. Taylor settled back on the couch and drew Beck close again. "Now, where was I?"

"Right here." She raised her lips to his. She didn't need Claudette Colbert and Clark Gable for inspiration. Everything she needed was right here in Taylor's arms.

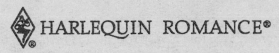 **HARLEQUIN ROMANCE®**

brings you

Stories that celebrate love, families and children!

Watch for our next Kids & Kisses title in October.

**Sullivan's Law
by Amanda Clark
Harlequin Romance #3333**

A warm, engaging Romance about people you'll love and a place that evokes rural America at its best. By the author of A Neighborly Affair *and* Early Harvest.

Jenny Carver is a single parent; she works too hard and worries too much. Her son, Chris, is a typical twelve-year-old—not quite a kid anymore but nowhere near adulthood. He's confused and bored and resentful—and Jenny isn't sure how to handle him. What she decides to do is take him to Tucker's Pond in Maine for the summer—a summer that changes both their lives. Especially when they meet a man named Ben Sullivan....

Available wherever Harlequin books are sold.

MILLION DOLLAR SWEEPSTAKES (III)

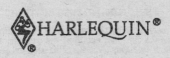

THE VENGEFUL GROOM
Sara Wood

Legend has it that those married in Eternity's chapel are destined for a lifetime of happiness. But happiness isn't what Giovanni wants from marriage—it's revenge!

Ten years ago, Tina's testimony sent Gio to prison—for a crime he didn't commit. *Now* he's back in Eternity and looking for a bride. *Now* Tina is about to learn just how ruthless and disturbingly sensual Gio's brand of vengeance can be.

THE VENGEFUL GROOM, available in October from Harlequin Presents, is the fifth book in Harlequin's new cross-line series, **WEDDINGS, INC.** Be sure to look for the sixth book, **EDGE OF ETERNITY,** by Jasmine Cresswell (Harlequin Intrigue #298), coming in November.

WED5

HARLEQUIN SUPERROMANCE®

Newsflash! Ellen James to be published by Superromance!

If you've enjoyed Romance books by Ellen James—like *The Confirmed Bachelor*—you'll love *Tempting Eve*!

Tempting Eve is Ellen's first Superromance, and you can buy it in September wherever Harlequin books are sold.

ELLENJ

MIRA™

The brightest star in women's fiction!

This October, reach for the stars and watch all your dreams come true with **MIRA BOOKS**.

HEATHER GRAHAM POZZESSERE
Slow Burn in October
An enthralling tale of murder and passion set against the dark and glittering world of Miami.

SANDRA BROWN
The Devil's Own in November
She made a deal with the devil...but she didn't bargain on losing her heart.

BARBARA BRETTON
Tomorrow & Always in November
Unlikely lovers from very different worlds... They had to cross time to find one another.

PENNY JORDAN
For Better For Worse in December
Three couples, three dreams—can they rekindle the love and passion that first brought them together?

The sky has no limit with **MIRA BOOKS**.

This September, discover the fun of falling in love with...

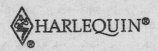

Harlequin is pleased to bring you this exciting new collection of three original short stories by bestselling authors!

ELISE TITLE
BARBARA BRETTON
LASS SMALL

LOVE AND LAUGHTER—sexy, romantic, fun stories guaranteed to tickle your funny bone and fuel your fantasies!

Available in September wherever Harlequin books are sold.

 HARLEQUIN®